Sharkes
in the
North Woods

Sharkes in the North Woods

or

Nish Na Bosh Na Is Nicer Now

Jane Zaring

Houghton Mifflin Company
Boston

Library of Congress Cataloging-in-Publication Data

Zaring, Jane.
   Sharkes in the north woods, or, Nish Na Bosh Na is nicer now.
   Summary: Four campers, trapped at a summer camp run by the Sharke family, plan a daring escape when the Sharkes hold the entire camp for ransom.
   ISBN 0-395-32271-5
   [1. Camping—Fiction. 2. Crime and criminals—Fiction. 3. Kidnapping—Fiction]
I. Title
PZ7.Z264Sh   82-6096
[Fic]   AACR2

Printed in the United States of America

HC ISBN 0-395-32271-5
PA ISBN 0-395-56154-X

AGM 10 9 8 7 6 5 4 3 2 1

For Abigail, Andrew, David and Noah

Prologue

By the time Laura Lewis and her cousin Harry realized they were on the wrong road in the North Woods, things were clearly amiss with Nish Na Bosh Na. But the story didn't start there. Looking back, Laura was inclined to think that it began with the unlucky chance that drew her mother's eyes to the advertisement in the Chicago evening paper. In fact, it had started well before then, with Aunt Adelaide's original camp, Nellie Highly's rabid wolves, Egbert Sharke's forged checks, Coralene Sharke's brainwave, the sewage problems at Minor Falls, and the shady Mr. James Dubious. The best way to make sense of all this may be to begin before Laura left Chicago, with the first visit of Egbert Sharke and his horrible sisters to the North Woods . . .

1

―――――――

"One awaits the day," said Coralene Sharke, as the elderly VW bus rattled and bumped along a barely visible track, "when we are driven along this road in a pink Cadillac." She practiced a gracious wave of the hand to the passing trees.

The farther they had gone into the dark, dripping, barely thawed woods, the more pleased Coralene had looked. When her brother, Egbert, got out to discover whether the road went over, under, or around a thicket of energetic briars, a well-satisfied smile crossed her face. It sat a little oddly on her normally sour features.

Ten miles of jolts and swerves to avoid ruts and potholes had, however, done nothing for the temper of the driver, Egbert Sharke.

"And about time, too," he growled, as the bus took a right-hand bend around a stand of rusty cedars and came to a stop outside the main cabin of a sad-looking summer resort.

3

"All that way for this crummy hole. Coralene, you're nuts," he said.

His elder sister, Coralene, the organizer of the expedition, stepped out in her turquoise velvet polyester pantsuit, with dyed-to-match spike-heeled shoes. She shook back her glossy artificial curls and adjusted the mangy fox fur that ran tail-in-mouth around her neck.

"Perfect. Perfectly perfect," she cooed in silvery tones cold enough to send a curious chipmunk straight back into hibernation.

There was a rattle and a crash behind her, as the door of the bus was flung open and the third Sharke, Diana-Discipline, sprang out to stand beside her sister. Together, they looked like ill-matched peas from a family pod that ran to large noses and small eyes. Diana-Discipline inhaled some forceful gulps of the late March air, which was blowing a faintly rancid odor across the small lake, and took off at a jog through the woods, swerving to stamp on the first signs of green, where early spring flowers were struggling through the chilly ground. Before long, Coralene could see her thundering along the lake shore, poking her sizable nose into each of the decrepit, sagging cabins.

"Three leaking roofs, five broken doors, and seven windows gone," she reported on her return. "Plenty of spiders. Lots of mice. No plumbing working. I do think we are going to have a jolly summer here, Coralene. I've started tramping down the weeds."

"Jolly wasn't the precise word we had in mind,"

4

retorted her sister, who liked to speak of herself in the plural. She felt it hinted at unseen forces at her command. "However, the place will suit us very nicely indeed. It's just what we need, delightfully difficult to get into—and out of. Speaking of which, it's time we were getting back to Basswood."

She turned and looked at the bus with distaste. The rainbow painted on the back was now splashed and grubby. Stickers in various places posed questions and made suggestions: HAVE YOU HUGGED YOUR KID TODAY? HONK IF YOU'RE HAPPY. TRY SUNPOWER. Coralene shuddered.

"What disgusting sentiments. Let us hope we never have to meet the previous owners of this vehicle. Surely you could have found something better, Egbert? One does have to think of one's image, you know."

"Image," snorted her brother from the driver's seat. "That's rich. Here's Coralene looking for a hideout after her last confidence trick crashed; Diana-Discipline, fired as the Iowa State Boys' Reform School athletic coach; and yours truly, a forger out on parole. Don't talk to me about image, just be thankful this jalopy runs, my girl. You have to take what you can get in the lousy backwoods in winter."

"Beggars can't be choosers," trilled Diana-Discipline between the pushups she was busily doing on what had once been a terrace in front of the main cabin.

Coralene sent her a look of intense dislike. "Don't be tiresome, Diana. There will be plenty of time for exercises later. We have to see the real-estate man now."

Egbert turned the bus, craning his neck to see around the large dog that sat beside him. He had not left his seat, since he was allergic to fresh air.

"Calls itself a road?" he grumbled, dabbing his nose with a purple Kleenex as they lurched and swayed back to town and their appointment with the senior partner of Highly, Highly, Dubious & Smart, "Minnesota's Most Trusted Real Estate Agency."

2

Mr. James Dubious folded his hands on his over-stuffed stomach and looked discreetly at the ceiling. A glance in the strategically placed mirror told him that the lady opposite was indeed writing out a check for fifty thousand dollars. He had named that outrageous sum hoping to strike a bargain at half the amount. After all, the place had been on the books since before he had joined the family firm.

"What a lucky break," he thought to himself. "Just when I can use the money."

James Dubious, "Minnesota's most trusted real estate agent," was confident that a few carefully placed bribes could divert a new four-lane highway to Gooseberry and Little Fool lakes, which were located in one of the last remaining wilderness areas. Once the road came through, the holiday condominiums he planned should sell like hotcakes. Should he change the name to Swan Lakes? They said a rare pair of Trumpeter swans nested there. He made a mental note to see that when the trees were chopped down, one was left standing to hold the sign. SWAN LAKES in flashing neon lights was what he fancied. If those darned birds took a dislike to noise and abandoned the place he would have plastic replicas made. In fact, artificial swans would be far better: clean, quiet, and unlikely to attack the vacationers.

"Finished, Mrs. Sharke?" he asked. "Such a pleasure to do business with you. I always did admire a woman who could make her mind up on the spot. So rare in the fair sex."

Diana-Discipline drew herself up indignantly. He went on hastily, without giving her time to object.

"So wise of you to come up early and steal a March on the market. Ha, ha. Pardon my little joke. Seriously, at the rate property is selling in the North Woods, that little gem wouldn't have been around many more weeks."

Mr. Dubious crossed the fingers holding his cigar.

"My clerk will slip across to the courthouse to get the papers finalized. Then you can be on your way to view your fine new purchase. Old Camp Nish Na Bosh Na! I know you'll love its air of yesteryear. Such a relief amid the hustle and bustle of the modern world."

"Thank you. We have already inspected the property," said Coralene Sharke, tightening one turquoise-and-pink drop earring and shaking out the frills of her orange nylon blouse.

Mr. Dubious was surprised. He couldn't imagine anyone who had actually seen the place wanting to buy it.

"Aha! The handyman's challenge," he said with a merry laugh in the direction of Egbert's pale face and long, dripping nose.

Egbert tossed another purple Kleenex at the wastebasket and missed again.

"And what does your charming family plan to do with your new retreat?" asked James Dubious, smoothly changing the subject.

"We thought of communing with nature," Coralene said.

Egbert sniggered.

"I always feel nature is so pure in the North Woods, don't you, Mr. Dubious?" simpered Coralene.

"Absolutely pure," purred the realtor. "Just what I always say. My dear lady, you have the soul of a poet."

The three people in front of him didn't look like your average poets and nature lovers, but if their money was good (and his clerk was checking that at this very minute), then James Dubious was not one to ask awkward questions. He tilted his chair back and said, "Good doggie," to distract his clients' unattractive hound from the desk leg it was chewing. The dog slobbered on his expensive suede shoes instead.

"Why did that Camp Nish Na Whatsit fold?" asked Diana-Discipline abruptly.

"Ah, Miss Sharke, what a sharp question! Well now, let me see. It was before my day, but I did hear there was some scare about rabid wolves. Not a word of truth in it, of course, but the rumor was enough to scuttle the camp. Parents are funny creatures."

9

"And why has the place not been sold since?" Diana-Discipline went on relentlessly.

Mr. Dubious squirmed in his swivel seat and glanced at the check, now lying securely on his side of the desk. The date and signature seemed to be in order. He casually put his hand over it, in case the Sharkes decided to withdraw their offer.

"It seems," he admitted, "people got the idea that the sewage from a nearby town, Minor Falls—such a picturesque spot—was draining directly into the lake. An unfounded notion, naturally, but you know what people are. My dear old auntie," he continued, trying to steer the conversation into safer, more sanitary waters, "used to go to Camp Nish Na Bosh Na as a girl. She always thought most highly of it. Not surprising, as she was a Highly. Nellie Highly. Ha, ha!"

"Quite the joker, Mr. Dubious," Coralene observed acidly.

"Yes. Well, the place was famous in its day. I believe my aunt even hoped to take it over, but it was always run by Adelaide Lewis, the well-known educator. She was forever trying something new: boys and girls at the same camp, growing their own food, Greek dancing, yoga, Indian knots, all that sort of thing. Are you thinking of starting the old camp up again?"

"No, no," said Coralene Sharke hastily.

"Yes, yes," said Diana-Discipline Sharke.

"That's the ticket," said Egbert, laughing nastily behind his handkerchief. "Two stories for the price of one."

"Perhaps a teeny-weeny start," amended Coralene. "I think we can let you in on the secret, Mr. Dubious. The truth is, we hope to give some children a much-needed holiday in the fresh air. My sister is absolutely dedicated to maladjusted youngsters, and my brother and I are lending a hand with her mission of mercy. But we must beg you, Mr. Dubious, not to mention it to anyone. The children are extremely disturbed, and any interruption in their day could undo all our good work. So we must discourage any visitors."

"What a rare pleasure to meet noble souls who sacrifice worldly pleasures without the fanfare of publicity," said Mr. Dubious without blinking an eye.

Coralene lowered her own rather small eyes modestly. Diana-Discipline stared disapprovingly at the realtor's waistline.

"My good man, you are appallingly out of shape," she said. "You should quit cigars and eat sensibly; spinach, celery, that's the stuff. And you should run, run, run."

Mr. Dubious tightened his grasp on his cigar and greeted the return of his clerk with some relief.

"That puts everything in order. Here are the deeds. You will want to be off right away. And," he added, looking sincerely into Coralene's eyes, "I just know you will be very, very happy in your own little corner of our great state."

Mr. Dubious was proud of his sincere look. He had every right to be. He had practiced it long and hard in front of his bathroom mirror.

11

That night Mr. Dubious told his wife, as he polished off a third helping of banana-coconut cream pie, "Made an easy buck today, Tootsie. Some real screwballs bought the old Nish Na Bosh Na place. I gather they're going to keep criminal kids there or something. Anyway, they want it pretty hush-hush. If you ask me, the man (a nasty piece of work if ever I saw one) wants to lie low for a bit."

"Well, heavenly days," said Mrs. Dubious. "I must certainly tell Aunt Nellie. She always seemed to feel real bad about the old camp shutting down. I don't suppose it matters about the contaminated water, James? After all, criminal kids are probably used to things like that."

"Sure," agreed her husband, "kids drink anything. Now if I can only get old Miss Lewis to sell me her five acres on the other side of Minor Falls, we'll be sitting pretty. I've bought up the rest of the Gooseberry and Little Fool area cheaply, since no one knows about the road. But the Lewis property controls the way in; I've got to have it."

"But Pootsie, she has never allowed any development there."

"I know, Tootsie. She's a tough nut to crack. Is there any of that pie left? I believe I'll have another helping."

3

————

"Yes, that will do nicely," said Coralene Sharke, turning from her seat at the dressing table in a room at the Blue Loon Motel, where she was busy typing a brochure for the camp the Sharkes intended to run that summer. Properly done, she felt, it should provide the the three of them with more money than they had made in all their previous schemes combined. But first, Coralene had to attract the right kind of children: the ransomable kind, whose wealthy parents could be relied upon to stay at a distance in June and July, and to come through with the money in August. She began to read her list of camp attractions to Egbert and Diana-Discipline. *"Energy Conservation. Character-Building Experience."*

"Change that to road-building experience," suggested Egbert, idly practicing various signatures, none his own, in soap on the bathroom mirror.

"Thank you, dear boy," said his sister. "I'll make that *Road-Building for the Future*. No one will believe we mean it the hard way. I guess handling a pick and shovel covers *Muscle Development* and *Practical Self-Reliance*." She penciled them in. "Now what else?"

"Food," suggested Diana-Discipline, gnawing an apple.

"Ah yes, I have it down. *Sound Nutrition. Sugar-Free Diet*."

"Wait a minute," said Diana-Discipline, aiming the core at the mirror and smearing one of Egbert's masterpieces. "We haven't got a cook."

"Yes we have: you," replied Coralene promptly.

"You've got to be kidding. I always burn the toast, and I've never even boiled an egg or mashed a potato in my life."

"All the more reason for starting now," said Coralene sweetly. "You know we can't cut anyone else in on this little scheme."

"When I think how the ribs of those pudgy little monsters are going to be sticking out after two weeks of your cooking, I almost pity them," said Egbert.

"Good idea," said his sister and wrote down *Weight Loss*.

"Let me think . . . what are we missing? I know. *Democratic Principles*."

"Democratic, my foot," snorted Egbert, wiping the mirror clean and starting afresh. "With old Di here running the place, it will be 'Heil Sharkey' and goose-stepping to breakfast."

"You have a point. I'll change that to *A Sensible Framework of Rules*. Thank you, Egbert. You are being unusually helpful. Now, does *Healthy* or *Health-Giving* sound better?"

"That reminds me. I want my cabin at least a hundred yards from that sewage," demanded Egbert.

"You always were a selfish mama's boy," observed Coralene, "and age hasn't changed you one bit. There is only one sound cabin, and, as director, I'm entitled to it. You can enjoy the waterfront. Please don't interrupt my train of thought again. *Close to Nature.*"

"Close to nature. With that stink? That's cool, that is," sneered Egbert. "Am I supposed to paddle in the stuff? Remember you promised me windows with glass in them for my allergy when I agreed to come."

"If you insist," grumbled his sister.

"Why not put *Home Away from Home* while you're about it?" asked Egbert, with heavy sarcasm.

"Why not, indeed?" said Coralene, and in it went. "Now tell me, have we included everything parents want for their children, but couldn't face for themselves?"

"*First-Class Gymnastic Training by Ex-Olympic Hopeful,*" suggested Diana-Discipline. "*Long-Distance Running.*"

"Long-distance running! Are you out of your mind? The very last thing we want," snapped her sister.

"Kids might escape," explained Egbert to Diana-D, who was looking baffled.

"This heading is bothering me," continued Coralene, tapping her pencil on her mildly crossed front teeth. "It lacks zip. *Experimental Living with Nature. A Brand-New Experience for Outstanding Young People.*

15

Perhaps we should drop the 'experimental'? What do you think, D-D?"

"I'd like to see a bit about building healthy minds in healthy bodies," replied her sister, leaning against the closet to do a series of isometric exercises. "Why say 'brand-new'? Remember what that fat, oily real-estate man said about Nish Na Bother Its being famous in its day? I think we would attract far more kids if we pretended the old camp was reopening."

"Now that's very sharp," said Coralene handsomely. "Diana-Discipline, your bright ideas, unlike mine, may be few and far between, but once in a while you come up with a real humdinger. Let me try that in caps."

FOR ONE SEASON ONLY: REOPENING OF DISTINGUISHED SUMMER CAMP

"It looks great," said Coralene.

Diana-Discipline beamed. Coralene went on, inspired.

"Under that we'll put, *Since 1933 Nish Na Bosh Na has provided a character-building experience in group living for boys and girls with leadership potential.* That should get them. They'll be begging to sign up. I'll have to be Adelaide Lewis— Adelaide Coralene Lewis Sharke, the well-known educator."

"You are so clever, Coralene," said Diana-Discipline admiringly.

"We know," replied Coralene. "Let's hope the real Adelaide Lewis doesn't give us any trouble. She must be about a hundred, if she's still alive."

When Coralene was at last satisfied with her efforts, she interrupted the situps her sister had just started, to request that she take the brochure down to the Kopy Kwik and run off five hundred copies. Diana-D bounded out the door, but returned a moment later with a puzzled frown.

"But Coralene, how are we going to equip the camp? That fifty grand was all the money I had, and with your bankruptcy and poor Egbert's trouble, who's going to lend us any cash?"

"Oh, we'll think of something," replied her sister airily. "Garage sales, rejects, Spartan living."

Diana-Discipline left, still frowning.

"Now, Egbert," said Coralene, turning her attention to her sulking brother. "You simply have to rename that dog. She is going to be most useful to us, but Dopey is quite out of the question."

The big dog lifted her head on hearing her name. Egbert rubbed her stomach with his foot.

"If I rename my dog, your ladyship, you'd better be sure your fancy scheme works," said Egbert. "I'm not going to the trouble of retraining her for nothing."

"When we set our mind to something, it works," declared his sister, with a royal toss of the head.

"Just as well your teeth are crossed when you say that," said her brother, unimpressed.

4

Laura Lewis was helping her mother pack for a concert tour in Europe. It was the end of June, and if Laura had had any inkling of Mr. Dubious's real-estate dealings three months earlier, or of the peculiar guests in the Blue Loon Motel, she would not have been so calm about leaving the safety of their Chicago apartment.

"Darling, I do wish you were going with me," wailed her mother for the umpteenth time, looking helplessly at her half-packed luggage.

"Now, Mother. You know perfectly well we couldn't afford it. We've already spent your summer earnings on the grand piano and my braces," replied Laura, suppressing the thought that there was nothing she would like better. "Besides, I haven't got a passport. That black sweater goes in the far pile. Look, here are safety pins in case your zipper breaks again."

"Thank you, darling. You think of everything. Laura, I do feel guilty about your having stayed here and missed the first two weeks of camp."

"Don't worry, Mother. It was much nicer spending the two weeks here with you, and it worked out better for Cousin Harry too, didn't it?"

Lydia Lewis looked gratefully at her daughter, who was bending over a suitcase, untamed brown curls flying in every direction and hazel eyes directed on the job at hand. Her heart turned over in tenderness as she thought how like poor Steven Laura was. Aloud she said, "It's lucky you take after your father, sweetheart. Two scatty ones in the family would be an impossibility."

Laura looked up with a brief grin and said, "I know." She continued to go down her checklist: money, shoes, hairbrush, tickets, music. Her mother was catching a plane for London — that is, if Laura got her off in time. Laura was remarkably efficient. She knew that this quality earned her few friends at school. Some people even called her Miss Bossy behind her back. Still, it seemed to her that since her father's death, it was her job to see that the household didn't come unglued.

Mrs. Lewis paced the living room. "What if the tour is a total fiasco?"

"It won't be, Mother. You know you sing beautifully. Everyone says so."

"Thanks, but I shall be worrying about you, too, my sweet."

"Oh, I shall be perfectly safe polishing my leadership potential in the North Woods. Remember what the brochure said? 'Camp Nish Na Bosh Na strives to build both character and muscles.' Think how

19

much more suitable character-building in northern Minnesota is for a growing girl than late nights, hotel rooms, restaurant meals, and airports," said Laura, wishing once more that she was going with her mother.

"Well, Nish Na Which What certainly sounds a little high-minded for my taste, all that self-sufficiency and sound nutrition. If your father hadn't been so fond of the place, I should never be sending you off to a strange camp."

"Don't worry, Mother. It isn't exactly strange if Great-Aunt Adelaide is running it. What is she like?"

"I've never actually met her, but your father thought she was wonderful. Apparently she believed strongly in getting back to the land, and has lived for years in northern Minnesota, miles and miles from anywhere, without a telephone or even a mailbox, so far as I can tell. She was very fond of your father, and wrote me such a nice letter when he died, but I haven't heard from her since, not even this summer—which is odd, though I expect she has written to your uncle Hal. When they were boys, your father and he used to have a marvelous time at her camp. I was surprised she opened it up again, because she must be quite old by now."

"It's lucky you spotted that advertisement in the newspaper saying Miss Adelaide Lewis's famous camp was reopening," said Laura, rather wishing her mother hadn't. "I wonder why she didn't write to tell us that's what she was doing? And I do think she might have replied to the news that her long-lost great-niece and -nephew are coming to her precious camp. You didn't by any chance throw away her letter, did you?"

Mrs. Lewis had a habit of sweeping the mail that piled up on her desk into the wastebasket.

"I doubt it, darling," said her mother vaguely. "I usually look. But that's the big point, isn't it? You won't be alone there." She cheered up at the thought. "I'm delighted you'll meet your cousin Harry at last. Sending the pair of you to Aunt Adelaide's camp has to be the brainwave of the year. It's perfectly ridiculous that you and Harry don't know each other. You ought to know your own kith and kin. But with your uncle Hal always off on mysterious missions to remote parts of the world, I began to despair of your ever getting together. It's lucky that Aunt Jo was looking for somewhere for young Harry to spend the summer vacation."

The airport taxi arrived, as usual, before anyone expected it. There was a minor panic when Mrs. Lewis couldn't find her passport and traveler's checks. Laura retrieved them from a pile of stuff on the kitchen counter and touched the wooden chopping block for luck before waving her mother off. Then she got to work with her usual dispatch. She had already stowed the cat and the key with neighbors and put the plants on the balcony to take their chances, when the phone rang. It was her mother at the airport.

"Darling, I'm awfully sorry, but I seem to have brought my addresses for the next two months with me, the ones I meant you to have in Minnesota.

I thought I had left them on the kitchen counter for you. What shall we do?"

"Send them to Camp Nish Na Bosh Na, Mother."

"Good idea. I'll mail them before I get on the plane. Be sure to write."

"I will."

"Darling, I think I would forget my head if you weren't there. You know, I might have thrown Aunt Adelaide's letter away after all. That would explain her silence, wouldn't it? Goodness, that's my flight being called. Love to Aunt A, and Harry. Have a good time. Bye."

Laura hung up the phone with renewed misgivings about her mother's ability to manage on her own. Then, glancing at the clock, she stuffed some shorts and shirts into her backpack, along with a toothbrush and her handy Swiss army pocketknife, checked the windows, locked the door, and walked smartly down to the Greyhound bus station. She hoped she was going to like the cousin she was due to meet in six hours in Basswood, Minnesota. She also hoped, with less optimism, that she was going to enjoy Aunt Adelaide's character-building camp, run according to Olympic standards. Laura's character seemed okay to her; nothing to brag about, but not especially in need of building, either. The wilds of Minnesota seemed almost as far from Chicago as Europe did, and a whole lot less promising.

5

In the Basswood bus station, Cousin Harry stuck out like a Brussels sprout in a flower bed. Everybody there seemed to be taking some interest in the arrivals and departures. But Harry—Laura knew it had to be him—was hunched over an atlas of the Second World War. There wasn't a great deal of him to be seen, since he wore a khaki second lieutenant's hat, several sizes too large, pulled low over his eyes. Below that was an oversized dark blue sweat shirt with an enormous yellow *A* on the front. His knees, looking rather pale and unused to daylight, emerged from a pair of scout shorts. His feet, in scruffy sneakers, rested firmly on his backpack, so that no one could make off with it while its owner's attention was elsewhere.

Harry didn't look up as Laura approached, even when she stood directly in front of him. He seemed to be studying with a surprising degree of interest the area held by the Allied troops at 2400 hours on D-day. Laura decided it was lucky that one of them was operating in the bus station of Basswood, Minnesota, rather than in Occupied France; otherwise the chances of their arriving at Great-Aunt Adelaide's camp would be slim. She leaned toward him and said, "*A* for attention."

Harry looked up, startled. For a moment his gray eyes looked blankly into her hazel ones, and then a rueful smile transformed his narrow, serious face.

"You must be Laura. Sorry I didn't see you."

"And you are the famous, unknown Harry," she returned cheerfully. "What a neat hat."

"Well, I have to tell you about that," said Harry, looking a bit guilty. He had planned to work up to this point slowly. "The hat was your dad's, so it really belongs to you. Would you like to have it back?"

He held it out to her. Laura could see how much he valued the hat and what it cost him to make the offer, and she was touched by his honesty.

"No thanks. I'm sure my father would have been glad to see you using it. Besides, it would look a bit funny on me. Where did you find it?"

"It was at the back of a cupboard at home. It's got your father's name inside—Steven Lewis. Dad said I could have it, since my middle name is Steven, after him, you know. He said they liked to play war games as boys."

Harry's voice trailed off as he wondered if it was tactful to remind his cousin of her father. Laura thought how strange it was that this boy's father, her uncle Hal, whom she barely remembered, probably knew more about her father than she herself did.

She didn't like to think about that, so she looked up at the bus-station clock.

"It's nearly four. My mother asked if someone from Aunt Adelaide's camp could pick us up at five. Let's look around Basswood for an hour. It seems a waste to spend the time breathing in bus exhaust," she said.

Harry replaced the cap, much relieved that his cousin seemed so reasonable, and started stuffing the pile of books beside him into his backpack. Laura noted *Fighter Pilots of the Pacific War*, *Great Land Battles*, *Duel of the Ironclads*, *Famous Wartime Escapes*, and *Heroes of the Spartan Wars*.

"Hey, this is going to be a nice, peaceful self-reliance project, organized by our distinguished great-aunt. I don't think you need to read up on battles as preparation—at least I hope not."

Harry grinned again. Laura decided he had rather a nice smile. He held out *A Field Track Guide to Minnesota Mammals* and *Plants and Trees of Our Minnesota Parks*. "I found these on the shelves at home and thought they might be handy. I don't only read war. I try a bit of peace now and then."

"Do you always get as lost in a book as you were just now?" asked Laura, who always knew what was going on around her.

"Sometimes. The bus I caught from Duluth Airport got here two hours ago. Basswood didn't look very friendly to me, so I buried myself in a book. I'm not sure I'm going to like going to camp—it was my parents' idea—and so I brought this stack of books to read. It won't last me all summer, but I expect they'll let us go into town to the library. You're welcome to borrow any of these."

Laura thanked him. Since they were quite likely to be bored with a sweet old great-aunt, it was a good offer. She smiled at him as they shouldered their packs and sauntered out into Basswood.

The main street curved up a gentle hill from the bus station, soon ran out of buildings, and disappeared into the trees. There was a sign indicating that the Basswood Historical Museum was ahead, so they started up the hill in search of it. The town no longer looked unfriendly to Harry, now that this determined cousin with the mop of curls was beside him.

They passed a gift shop that featured wooden loons perched on a branch of driftwood and some cheerful, hand-knitted fish, and then a place offering to print shirts with any one of five hundred designs.

"I think camps usually have their own T-shirts, so I expect we'll want to wear that," Laura predicted wrongly.

The bait and tackle store next door advertised moccasins, souvenirs, fishing licenses, and live bait. The cousins stopped to gaze at the prize catches of the week, which were displayed in an icebox in the window.

"Look," Harry pointed out. "It says that that big walleye was caught with a Shakespeare mouse. Do you think that's a real mouse? A Hamlet mouse?"

"Beats me," said Laura, reading the card above an enormous Great Northern pike.

They meandered on past a barbershop and Basswood Hardware.

26

"I do like this town," said Laura. "Let's come here from camp often."

Halfway up the hill, they came to a store advertising itself as an "Outfitter for Boundary Waters Canoe Expeditions." The display window held blankets and sleeping bags piled around a fake campfire. A real canoe and a huge stuffed pike were propped against the back wall. Laura and her cousin went inside. It turned out to be one of the most fascinating stores Laura had ever seen. High wooden counters held piles of flotation jackets, waders, mosquito repellent, flashlights, hunting knives. There were odd smells of kerosene, leather, varnish, and raw wool. No one asked what they wanted to buy, so Laura and Harry drifted from one delight to another until they ended up at the expedition-food counter.

"Amazing, all the meals you can pack into a small space," Laura said. She fingered a pouch of freeze-dried beef and looked at some slabs of carob cake. "Don't all these bars of energy stuff sound yummy?"

Harry agreed, and decided to buy an energy bar made of apricot, hazelnuts, and honey.

"The camp food may not be as good as all that," he pointed out, debating whether to eat the apricot bar then or save it for later.

"I don't see how they can possibly get a whole meal into one tube," commented Laura, examining a tube of spaghetti dinner.

"I bet this is the stuff they carry on army commando raids." Harry was so struck by this thought that he promptly bought the spaghetti dinner, a cube of beef stew, and a packet of carrot flakes. At the time, Laura was a little shocked at her cousin's extravagance, though she was to bless it later.

At the top of the hill, set back in a grassy area, was a small log building and a sign saying HISTORICAL MUSEUM.

"It's open this afternoon," said Laura, reading the notice pinned to the door. "And it's free. Come on."

Harry nodded agreeably, although he slipped a book out of his backpack just in case.

A strong smell of floor wax from the gleaming red linoleum made Laura wrinkle her nose at first as she worked her way past the old, brownish photographs of Indians and early logging operations, while Harry examined a large-scale geology map of the area. Laura moved on to look at the flowers and scrolls on the trunks brought from Finland by the earliest settlers in the area. She wondered if she would have been brave enough to pack all her possessions and sail from her home to a new world, as her own great-grandmother had done. She glanced happily around from the gigantic moose antlers to the first school desk. It was just the kind of place she liked, and apparently Harry did too; at least he had not opened his book, and was studying the geology map attentively.

She walked over to the woman sitting behind a typewriter and asked the time.

"Ten of five, honey," the woman replied.

It was time they were getting back to the bus station for their ride to Camp Nish Na Bosh Na. On the way,

28

they bought an English toffee ice apiece. Then they settled down to wait for Aunt Adelaide.

"The summer might not turn out so badly after all," thought Laura, licking her way around solid chunks of toffee.

6

A ramshackle VW bus drew up near the cousins. Laura watched as a most unattractive individual got out and stopped to light a cigarette. He had a pale, waxy face, with a moist, red, peculiarly sharp nose. Long wisps of lank yellow hair emerged from under a grubby, pearl-gray Stetson with an orange and brown feather headband, and covered the collar of a windbreaker that had certainly seen better days. The stranger threw down the empty pack and made off up the street, casting quick glances behind him, as if he expected to be followed.

"He certainly doesn't look as though he belongs with that cheerful rainbow bus, does he?" observed Laura, as the man disappeared into the post office.

Harry licked the bottom of his sugar cone reflectively and studied the bus.

"Maybe he stole it. That guy looks quite capable of stealing something. You know, I didn't want to come to this camp, but my dad has gone off to the

South Pacific, and my mother had a chance to join him in Fiji. So when your mother phoned to say she had seen an advertisement saying that Great-Aunt Adelaide was reopening her camp, they jumped at the idea. They said that I needed to get out of doors and that Aunt Adelaide was wonderful. Is she really all that great? It seems to me that the only good thing about this Nish Na Bosh Na is that we've missed the first two weeks."

"I know just how you feel," said Laura sympathetically. "I didn't want to come either. I really wanted to go to Europe as my mother's manager. Yes, manager. I could do it perfectly well," she said, squelching Harry's look of surprise.

The man from the VW bus came out of the post office with a bundle of letters and went into the drugstore.

"I bet that man has never been within a hundred miles of a camp in his life," Laura said. "He certainly looks as if he would loathe fresh air, exercise, and any kind of fun. Camps are supposed to be fun, so it may be all right after all."

Harry started reading the advertisements of Property for Sale in the window behind them. He had just got to "Dream-come-true condominium in the planned holiday community of Swan Lakes" when a portly man in a hurry came out of the office and bumped straight into him.

"Don't clutter the doorway. Doesn't anybody teach manners nowadays?" he said and waddled off without an apology.

"I wonder whether that charming character was Mr. Highly, Mr. Dubious, or Mr. Smart?" asked Harry, reading the sign above the office. Laura was beginning to realize that her cousin read anything in print, even signboards.

The pale man emerged from the drugstore with four boxes of Kleenex, and started walking toward them. Harry and Laura politely looked the other way until they could no longer ignore him.

"The carriage awaits, kiddos," he announced in a voice quite as repellent as his appearance.

"Thank you. We are waiting for our Aunt Adelaide to meet us," said Laura, turning a cold shoulder to the stranger.

"I may not be up to Your Highness's expectations, but that same 'Aunt' has sent me to collect you and your cousin Harry Lewis. And a lot of trouble you have given us by ignoring our letter telling you that we were full up and unable to accept you."

Laura's mouth dropped open. "But . . ."

"You can walk to the camp for all I care, but it is twenty miles or so, and there are wolves in the woods, my dear."

He smiled mirthlessly.

"Wolves. Don't be silly. They are almost extinct in North America," replied Laura crisply. This was one statement the awful man had made that she could deal with.

"Please yourself," said the man indifferently, extending a clammy hand for her pack. Laura backed away.

Harry came to her rescue. "Do you have evidence that our aunt has sent you to meet us? And what did you mean about the camp being full up?"

"Quite the little general, aren't we?" the odious man sneered. He thrust a paper at them, which proved to be a letter from Laura's mother, giving the time and date of their arrival at Basswood and requesting that someone meet them. Then he pulled out an envelope with Laura's mother's sprawling script on the front, and pointed to the address: Miss Adelaide Lewis, Camp Nish Na Bosh Na, Box 292, Basswood, Minnesota.

"See. All in order. We might not want you, but we couldn't have the famous singer Lydia Lewis's daughter wandering around Basswood and asking for Camp Nish Na Bosh Na, could we?"

"Schleswig-Holstein. I don't like the look of this one bit," muttered Harry as the driver went around to open his door.

"Perhaps it's difficult to get a good handyman, or whatever he is, all the way up here," whispered Laura, less confident than she tried to sound. "What's Schleswig-Holstein? I thought it was Nish Na Bosh Na."

"It's part of Germany. Just below Denmark. Geography is my favorite subject, so I sometimes say the names of places on the map like that, just to get my courage up."

"Hmm," said Laura, who didn't usually need to screw up her courage.

The driver got in and started the bus after a few misfires. He swung around to face the children.

33

"Perhaps I had better introduce myself. I am Egbert Sharke. Sharke with an *e*—always remember the *e*—Director of Cultural Programs, Chief Medical Consultant, Handwriting Coach Extraordinaire, and Co-owner of Camp Nish Na Fishy Na, and here in the front seat beside me is Dope—er, Danger. Say 'hello,' Danger."

The enormous dog in the front passenger's seat bared an alarming set of yellow fangs and dripped a Niagara of saliva down the back of the seat.

7

The two children sat in the back of the bus, as far from Mr. Sharke and Danger as they could manage. Laura forgot her misgivings for a while as she caught enticing glimpses of lakes through the woods. She had never seen so many trees and so few people in her life. All she could see were trees, trees, and more trees, with now and again a gleam of water.

At first, only the road itself, and the telephone poles that ran alongside, told Laura that the area was inhabited, though gradually she began to spot mailboxes and signboards where narrow dirt side roads turned off to unseen dwellings. They passed a rock-strewn pasture grazed by a few red-brown cattle and two piebald horses. At the edge of the wood there was an abandoned log house, and nearer the road the house trailer that had replaced it, mounted on concrete blocks and buttressed by a large woodpile. The little farm was divided into small hayfields, scattered with clumps of birch and piles of rocks cleared from the rest of the land. Laura glanced at her cousin to see if he was as fascinated by this unfamiliar scenery as she was. Harry was looking more and more troubled.

"Excuse me," he said to the driver at last. "You must be going in the wrong direction. The brochure clearly said twenty miles south of Basswood, and we are going north."

"It's all these trees," returned Mr. Sharke. "They get a little lad all mixed up over north and south, east and west, and top and bottom."

"But I can see the sun over on my left," persisted Harry, seething at the patronizing tone. "It should be on my right if we were going south."

"Ever hold a map upside down, Lieutenant?" asked the pale man with a sneer.

"I know I'm right," muttered Harry to Laura. "I tried to find the position of the camp on that map in the museum. Nish Na Bosh Na didn't seem to be marked at all, but I saw enough of the lie of the land to be certain we are headed for the Canadian border at the moment."

"In that case," whispered Laura, alarmed by this intelligence, "we had better try to remember some landmarks, so we can find our way back, if necessary."

They tried to memorize the route for a while, but the road twisted and turned around seemingly identical lakes, and between stands of spruce, pine, and birch that were hopelessly alike.

"I give up," said Laura. "But at least we have the Sharke version of a trail of little white pebbles."

They giggled, realizing that the story of Hansel and Gretel, lost in the forest, had crossed both their minds because Egbert Sharke had been sneezing and tossing used tissues out of the window ever since they had left Basswood.

"And remember that we are going to meet Aunt Adelaide instead of the wicked witch," Laura went on, feeling a surge of her usual common sense.

Harry looked unconvinced, and began to search for a book in his pack.

"Look at those rolls of hay," said Laura, trying to find something to think about besides their plight.

"They look exactly like Tootsie Rolls," decided Harry, looking up from the index of his book. "Here, look at this," he added.

He handed Laura his field track guide and pointed to the place where it said "Gray Wolf. *Canis lupus*. Still found in small numbers in Canada and Alaska, rarely in northern Minnesota. Extremely shy. Tracks like dog."

Laura nodded vigorously as she read. "I knew he was lying about those wolves, but why? Just to scare us?" She hoped their strange driver would soon put them down at a cheerful, bustling camp and end her worries.

"Harry, what did Aunt Adelaide write to Uncle Hal? Did she really say the camp was too full to take us?"

"She didn't write to us. Dad assumed she had written to you."

"Then Mother must have lost the letter. Oh dear, I don't like this at all."

At long last, the bus swerved off the main road and stopped. Mr. Sharke got out to unfasten a chain across an apparently disused track, drove the bus forward a few paces, and stopped again. Swinging in the wind was a shiny new sign, saying in freshly painted letters:

CAMP
NISH NA BOSH NA
FOR

Then there was a gap, and on the bottom line it said

CHILDREN

Laura was relieved, and turned to reassure Harry. "It's all right. We're in the right place, thank goodness. It's awfully easy to get muddled about direction in a strange place."

Harry checked the position of the sun again. It was on their left. He shrugged his shoulders, pursed his lips, and looked mulish. Laura wondered if he was going to be so agreeable after all.

The camp's co-owner picked up a pot of red paint, a hammer and nails, and some signs that had been lying beside Danger on the front seat. He got out of the bus again. Laura caught sight of the top sign. It read DANGER. KEEP OUT.

Mr. Sharke hung it on the chain he had refastened across the road. Then he nailed another sign onto a balsam fir on one side of the track: WILD-LIFE PRE-SERVE. STRICTLY PRIVATE. TRESPASSERS WILL BE SHOT.

He took his hammer to the other side of the track and tacked a third sign to a young jack pine. This one said BEWARE RABID WOLVES.

Then, with swift strokes, he painted the word *Disturbed* on the swinging sign, and obliterated *Nish Na Bosh Na* with a sidelong swipe of Chinese red.

CAMP
FOR
DISTURBED
CHILDREN

read Laura, arching her eyebrows. Then an answer occurred to her, and she looked happier.

"I gather there are several camps along this trail?" she asked Mr. Sharke, as he revved up the stuttering engine once more.

"Oh no, princess," he answered with his odious chuckle. "Just one."

8

The drive along the bumpy road continued in apprehensive silence on the children's part while Egbert whistled a never-ending "How Much Is That Doggie in the Window?" to Danger, who drooled appreciatively. Eventually they pulled up amid a tumbledown collection of buildings beside a small, murky lake.

"This is the end of the line. Out you get, campers," announced Egbert with a snicker.

Laura got out and looked around in dismay. There were cabins without doors. There were cabins where thriving saplings peered out of empty windows. In some the roof sagged crazily, while in others the roof appeared to be entirely absent. Only one of the buildings was in good repair, and, as Egbert honked his horn impatiently, two women emerged from it. The children gazed at them in disbelief.

"Schleswig-Holstein," muttered Laura, trying out Harry's geographical method of getting up courage.

She crossed the fingers on both hands as well. The situation called for all the help she could get.

"Vladivostok," she heard Harry say behind her.

The leader of the two was small and fat, with glossy reddish curls bouncing on her shoulders as she walked toward them. Close up, her face, with its thick coating of powder, looked even worse than at a distance. It reminded Laura of a peach-colored mask. She had a sharp pointed nose, identical to Egbert's (though without the drip), small red-rimmed eyes shadowed in pearly green, and a mouth painted in an extravagant Cupid's bow of magenta lipstick. Two nobby brown warts on one rouged cheek and another on her chin drew Laura's eyes like magnets, no matter how hard she tried to avoid staring at them. The strong wave of perfume coming from the lady obliterated another smell that Laura had been trying to place ever since she got out of the VW bus.

Behind this beauty towered a gaunt, middle-aged woman with the family nose. The second woman's straight iron-gray hair was cut in flat bangs across her forehead. She wore a gray track suit with five Olympic rings clumsily sewn on the pocket. Around her neck an outsize whistle and five keys hung on a red cord. Laura never saw her without the keys and whistle the whole time she was at Nish Na Bosh Na. She must have slept with them on.

Both women looked far worse than your very worst imaginings of an unknown aunt.

"Here they are, unfortunately: the little princess and the gallant lieutenant, come to spend the summer with their ever-loving relatives," said Egbert, smirking as he pushed Laura and Harry forward.

The short fat one advanced.

"Dear Steven's little girlie," she cooed, pushing the warty cheek forward to be kissed. "We did so hope you wouldn't come."

Laura took a hasty step backward.

"Hmm. That's no way to greet your auntie," snapped the woman, presumably Great-Aunt Adelaide, in far more vinegary tones. She turned her attention to Harry.

"Mercy. What a shrimp!"

Harry flinched. Being taunted about his size was what he hated most.

"What a ridiculous hat," commented his tormenter. "And what did your dear father tell you about me?" she asked, turning back to Laura.

"I don't remember. He died several years ago," replied Laura truthfully. She almost thought the gaunt woman looked relieved, but her attention was distracted by the plump sister, who had seized one of Egbert's tissues and was dabbing her eyes.

"Of course, so sad. Sooo sad, sad, sad. Even now, just to think of it makes me weep." She began to sob noisily.

A moment later, making a remarkable recovery from her grief, she announced, "We have no time for family history, but I am your aunt Adelaide. Egbert and Diana-Discipline here are your step-cousins-in-law. My married name, in case your parents forgot to tell you, is Sharke, Adelaide Coralene Lewis Sharke.

I use Coralene nowadays. Adelaide is so hopelessly old-fashioned. You will both call me Mrs. Sharke, with an *e* of course. It would make the other children jealous if we gave you special privileges, and we strive to be one big happy family here, don't we, Diana-Discipline?"

"Sure thing," said Diana-Discipline, straightening up from some knee bends.

Laura's new-found relative, Aunt Adelaide Coralene Sharke-with-an-e, was wearing a surprising outfit for a self-reliance camp. It was a full-skirted lime-green polka-dot dress, with a pussycat bow at the neck. Spike-heeled coral sandals, a chartreuse head scarf, and a heliotrope clutch purse completed the unlikely ensemble. She noticed Laura's stare and preened herself.

"We fancy we bring a touch of glamour and femininity into what is otherwise a plain and simple summer for all you little sweetie-pies."

Coralene twirled around and started back to her cabin, throwing a last order over her polka-dotted shoulder. "Sister, take them away for Camp Nish Na Bosh Na's very own arrival ceremony."

9

The tall sister, obeying orders with alacrity, seized Harry and Laura's arms above their elbows with a powerful grip. She marched them along the muddy lakeside to a birch log cabin whose door hung open. Through the roof they could see patches of cloudy sky.

"First things first," announced Diana-Discipline. She handed each of them a pair of navy shorts and a gray sweater with "Iowa State Boys' Reform School" stamped back and front. "Put these on," she commanded.

"Thank you, but we have our own clothes," said Laura, looking with dismay at the worn-out, shapeless garments.

"Cut the argument and do as I say," barked their alleged step-cousin-in-law. "Look sharp. One, two, three . . ."

They got into the clothes, despising themselves for their lack of courage but reluctant to find out what happened when Diana-Discipline got to ten.

"You wouldn't want other children to feel unhappy because they can't afford the fancy things you have."

Laura was stung by the injustice of the remark. "I brought shorts, jeans, and sweat shirts. You can hardly call that fancy, can you?"

"Fancy is as fancy does," replied the woman, shaking out their pockets and scooping up the money.

"I will put this cash in the Camp Bank for safety. My brother Egbert is camp banker, so it will be quite secure. All your other things will go nicely in here."

With that, she tossed Laura and Harry's clothes and packs into a large, knotty pine closet that had a new door.

"But I must have my Swiss army knife," protested Laura, beginning to gather her wits. "I always carry it, and surely it's going to be useful in camp."

"You can't just take away our stuff like that," spluttered Harry, following Laura's example. "What about my books?"

"Just a temporary measure for safekeeping," said Diana-Discipline, "and to protect your eyesight, of course. Reading is very bad for the eyes."

Harry set his cap more squarely. Things looked grim, but Laura was glad to see that at least he had been allowed to keep that. She guessed Harry would find it a considerable comfort.

"Now then, just two more little items and you can go and join the gang."

She pulled Laura toward her, and before the girl realized her intention, there was a snip, snap, and Laura's hair was shorter by four haphazard inches.

"Much cooler and more comfortable, besides being better for working," she said, swiftly grabbing Harry's cap and tossing it, too, into the closet.

"B-but . . ." said Harry, outraged.

"You wouldn't want to be court-martialed for wearing an unauthorized uniform, would you?" Diana-Discipline said. She fastened the closet with a large new padlock. "And now, one last little ceremony of welcome to Nish Na Bosh Na. Look this way."

She took a photograph of each of them looking at the camera with a mixture of fury and bewilderment. It made a distinctive snapshot, as their parents were to find out.

"May I please have my cap back, Miss Sharke?" asked Harry, recovering a measure of courage. "And I would like a book, too."

"Oh dear," said Diana-D. "What a very bad habit. We shall have to cure you of that. No, don't thank me," she said as Harry opened his mouth to protest. "It will be my pleasure to help a little step-cousin-in-law. Jogging is the answer, and pushups, of course. I will prescribe plenty of both, to take your mind off military headgear and books. You realize that I was once nearly chosen for the Olympic gymnastic team, and I haven't read a book in ten years."

With that, she marched them back along the lake shore.

"You have the fresh-air dorm, you lucky boy," she announced, throwing Harry's sleeping bag down alongside several others on the floor of an old shelter,

46

which had shreds of a roof, four corner uprights, and no walls.

Laura heard him saying Omsk, Tomsk, and Vladivostok as she was hurried farther down the path.

10

"The whole summer here?" Laura said to herself incredulously as she sat alone on the rickety bunk assigned to her by Diana-Discipline, and poked at a clump of grass growing up through the rotten floorboards. Her words hung in the musty air of the dingy cabin. She wished passionately that her mother had never noticed that advertisement for Camp Nish Na Bosh Na.

Laura did not as a rule waste much time in wishing the past undone. So she frowned at the broken glass in the window and asked out loud, "Laura, what do we do now?"

She had found that when she felt uncertain or worried, a brisk talk to herself could often put things right. It did so now.

"Well, for one thing, we can't possibly stay here," herself replied.

"Right," said Laura. "I shall write and tell Mother that I am leaving for home by the first bus from

48

Basswood. Harry can stay with me in Chicago until his parents return. Mother might have warned me that we have such awful relatives."

Having decided that she only had to stay one night, Laura felt more cheerful, and looked around for clues as to the other campers. The cabin was curiously empty. There were three rusty bunk beds, four khaki sleeping bags, and absolutely nothing else—not even four toothbrushes. She was beginning to fear that she would be quite alone in the decrepit room, when the door swung open and three small girls filed in, followed by a taller one.

Laura found it difficult to tell them apart. They all had cropped hair, obviously Diana-Discipline's handiwork, and wore the same navy shorts and Iowa State Boys' Reform School sweat shirts that Laura herself had on. The chief difference between them and her, so far as she could tell, was that while she looked clean enough to pass muster, they were covered from toes to eyebrows with mud.

"Hi," said Laura uncertainly.

" 'Lo," muttered one of the children.

Three of them took no further notice of Laura. They flung themselves on their bunks and were asleep in an instant.

"Poor kids. They're exhausted from building that dock," explained the tall girl, who was about Laura's age and seemed more friendly than the others. She had large dark eyes in an oval face, and almost black hair, which she shook back as though it had until very recently been long. Her gray Reform School shirt was streaked with mud, and the sleeves stopped well above her wrists. Laura was fairly tall for her age, but this girl was a whole head taller.

"I'm glad you've come. We could use another pair of hands," she said.

"However did you get so dirty?" asked Laura.

"It's easy when you work all day in the mud at the edge of the lake."

"Don't you wash before going to bed?" inquired Laura, rather shocked.

"With what?" asked the girl.

"Well, soap and water, I suppose," replied Laura, thinking it an odd question.

"We don't have any soap, and it would be no use anyway. The plumbing doesn't work. We only have the clothes on our backs. She took everything else and locked it up as soon as we came."

Laura had no difficulty in identifying "she" as Diana-Discipline. It seemed that the camp's welcoming ceremony was the same for everybody.

"But however do you get clean?" asked Laura.

"On Saturday mornings she makes us all get into the lake in our clothes and swim around a bit. Then we get out, hang up our shorts and shirts, and do calisthenics until they dry. Then we put them on again. They do smell a bit funny from the lake water, but you get used to it."

"Never," said Laura with certainty. "How gross. Thank goodness I'm leaving this dreadful place tomorrow."

"That's what they all say," observed the girl, "but

none of them does. The Sharkes won't let you go, and you can't escape. We're miles and miles from anywhere, and the woods are full of ferocious wild animals. They say you would get lost and go round and round in circles until you die of exhaustion and they would never find your body."

"Nonsense," said Laura robustly. "The Sharkes can't keep us here against our will." She pushed out of her mind the memory of the sign Egbert had hung at the end of the road.

"You'll see," warned the girl. "Hey, you've got a tick on your neck."

Laura felt the back of her neck. There seemed to be a wart she didn't remember. She brushed it away. It didn't move.

"No, you can't get it off like that. Here, I'll do it for you. I'm used to pulling them off the others. Ticks dig their heads in, you know, and get all fat on your blood. The sooner you pull them off, the better. They're really gross when they get big."

"Yech," said Laura, her skin crawling all over as she looked quickly to see what else might have attached itself to her. "How disgusting. There's nothing like that in Chicago."

"There are lots of them here," said her adviser matter-of-factly. "I think they drop from the roof of the cabin or something. Some kids tried to make up a camp song that started 'Tickery tickery tock,' but Coralene made them stop. She was afraid they were having fun. Now, I guess you'd have to say the whine of the mosquito is our camp song."

"I can't believe—" Laura started to say when somebody blew a piercing blast on a whistle. The sleeping girls jumped out of their bunks and ran like deer. The friendly girl beckoned Laura to follow.

"My name's Gwen," she panted as they ran along the lake path. "Watch where you're going. That's poison ivy. It's all around here."

Laura swerved back onto the path. A moment later, the two girls took their places at the back of a line of grubby children.

"Cross your fingers we get some supper," said Gwen. "We should have been quicker."

11

Harry fell into line behind Laura. Behind him came a small boy with sandy hair and freckles who could not have been more than seven. He looked surprisingly upset at finding himself last. Laura was delighted to see a familiar, friendly face. "Can you believe this place?" she asked.

"Shh," said Gwen. "You're not allowed to talk."

"Why ever not?"

"Silence, Laura Lewis," called Diana-Discipline, clashing two saucepan lids together for emphasis. "There is to be no talking at mealtimes at Camp Nish Na Bosh Na."

"But Miss Sharke, what harm can it do?" asked Laura more bravely than she felt inside.

"We don't want to loiter over meals when there are so many self-reliance projects waiting to be done, do we?" said Diana-Discipline, screwing up her eyes and peering fiercely at Laura from under her bangs, and at the same time shaking her head as if she deeply disapproved of what she saw. "A little

53

self-denial builds character. I can see that your character is going to need special attention."

"You're lucky it isn't her sister," said Gwen out of the corner of her mouth. "It never does to attract their attention. Look at me."

Laura looked, and realized why her new friend was standing so oddly. By bending her knees, hunching her shoulders, and sort of sloping backward, Gwen no longer stood out above the rest of the children. Laura squared her own shoulders.

"Laura," she said to herself, "we are not afraid."

"N-no," herself agreed. "Everybody has peculiar relatives, and we will soon be saying goodbye to ours. Anybody can stand anything, if it's only for one night."

The line shuffled up to where Diana-Discipline was doling out the evening meal. She handed each child a bowl of stew, two slices of bread, and a raw, brownish parsnip. Laura sat down and looked at her bread. It had green, whiskery stuff on one side. She pushed it away from her.

"Don't you want it?" a boy asked her hopefully.

"Good gracious, no," said Laura.

The boy shot out a skinny, far-from-clean hand, grabbed both slices, and devoured them in three bites. Laura hoped they would not do him permanent harm.

"What's this stew?" she whispered to Gwen.

"Sluggish Liver," was the reply. "You can see the lumps of liver, and the kids say it contains slugs as well."

Laura put down her bowl, untasted. The same boy picked it up and gave her a look of gratitude mingled with surprise. She gnawed her parsnip unenthusiastically, not entirely sure it was better than nothing at all.

The small freckled boy behind Harry at the end of the line arrived at the stew pot only to be told that the supply had run out, and that it served him right for being so tardy. Laura could see he was struggling not to cry.

"Please, Miss Sharke, I didn't have any supper last night either."

"Well, Ames, you know our little game: every man for himself and the last one here is a rotten egg. You'll just have to be quicker tomorrow, won't you?" she said.

"But Miss Sharke," the child pleaded desperately, dashing away his tears with a muddy fist that left his face looking like a soccer field after a solid week of rain. "I'm always so tired from building the new road that I can't keep awake until supper, and the others get here before I do."

"Don't argue," said Diana-Discipline. "Excuses are the sign of a weak character, and I am sure your parents would not like to think that Ames Oakes the Fifth is deficient in character."

The small boy sat down defeated. Harry surreptitiously handed him a piece of bread. Gwen slid across the remains of her Sluggish Liver. Laura passed down a half-gnawed stump of woody parsnip.

A chipped enamel bowl was passed around for the

children to help themselves to the green stuff inside. Few did.

"What is it?" asked Laura with her eyebrows.

"Nettle and Dandelion Salad," replied Gwen, without moving her lips.

Diana-Discipline blew her whistle for attention. "Now that you've finished our nourishing and nutritious sugar-free meal, it is time for postcards home."

The children looked eager and hopeful for the first time, especially Ames Oakes the Fifth. Diana-Discipline distributed one card to each child. Behind her came a privileged camper who gave a pencil stub to every third person.

"Now then," said Miss Sharke, cracking a bony knuckle. "Speed and efficiency are our goals. Ready, steady, go!"

She clanged the saucepan lids, and the children started writing for dear life. Diana-Discipline carefully regarded her watch, a large one on a businesslike strap, that had been especially designed for clocking speed at athletic events. As soon as the second hand had swept around three times, she blew her whistle. The children with pencils promptly passed them to the person on their left and surrendered their cards. A second blast on the whistle yielded a second harvest of postcards. At the third blast, the helper came running along, collecting pencil stubs.

"But I haven't finished," said Laura, calmly writing another word.

The children gasped. Miss Sharke stopped counting the pencils, turning mottled scarlet. "Laura Lewis!"

she screeched. "Tomorrow I shall see you are placed on the spinach detail."

There was a low murmur of sympathy, quickly hushed as Diana-Discipline glared around her in search of offenders. Ames Oakes pretended to be tying up a shoelace in order to mutter at Laura's knees.

"Thanks for the parsnip. I'm sorry about the spinach. You can't talk back to any of them, you know."

"It's okay," Laura reassured him. "I'm not going to be here tomorrow. She can do her own spinach."

A delicious smell of steak frying drifted past the hungry campers. Laura turned to identify the source, and saw that the Sharke cabin door had opened and Coralene was mincing toward them. She held a bowl of strawberries in one hand, and was daintily dipping them in sugar with the other.

"We hadn't quite finished our dinner," she announced, "but we didn't want to keep you waiting one moment longer than necessary for your bedtime story. Now, my little sweethearts," she said, licking some sugar from her lips and throwing a squashed berry over her shoulder, watched by fifty hungry eyes. "We have heard about little Jane, who was scalped by hostile Indians in the Minnesota woods last year. (They simply hate our being here, my dears.) Have we told you about the pack of man-eating wolves who are thought to live in this area? Oh, yes. That was yesterday. Well, I think I should tell you the sad story of little Willie, who got lost in the woods, was bitten by a rabid skunk, and was never seen again."

She tied a baby-blue net scarf more securely over her ginger curls, and began the tale of Willie, the young camper who would wander in the woods, despite the warnings of adults who knew better.

"Now," she said briskly as she finished, "off to bed with you. I see it's seven o'clock already, and we all want to conserve energy by not using any lights, don't we?"

"Mrs. Sharke," asked one brave soul, "was there any mail?"

"Not a scrap, brat," said Coralene sharply. "I must ask you to stop pestering me for letters. Your parents have probably forgotten all about you."

"Aunt Adelaide," Laura spoke out, quaking inside, "I think there has been a dreadful mistake, and I wondered: would you kindly arrange a ride back to Basswood for Harry and me, first thing tomorrow?"

There was an electric silence. The only sound seemed to be the beating of Laura's heart. She wondered if it could be heard across the lake, like an Indian tom-tom. From the corner of her eye, she could see the other children huddling together for protection from the thunder and lightning that were surely about to strike. Coralene took a different tack, however.

"Dear little Laura-paura," she purred silkily. "I don't think you fully understand your situation. Your mother and your cousin's parents are thousands of miles away across the Atlantic and Pacific oceans. They left you children in my care for the whole summer, not just twenty-four hours of it. I gather from my morning's mail that you don't even know your mothers' addresses. We can't possibly let you go. It is our duty, disagreeable perhaps, but our clear auntly duty, to keep you and Harry here in plain sight."

"Well, let me phone some friends of ours. They will be glad to look after us," urged Laura, beyond caution in her anxiety to get away from this horrible place.

"Certainly not. There is no phone here, even supposing we would allow you to use it. And you might be interested to know that there is no telephone within miles and miles of Nish Na Bosh Na," was the chilling reply.

12

Harry couldn't sleep. He usually read in bed until his eyes closed or his mother took the book away. Even now he felt around in the darkness, in the wild hope that his hands would meet a familiar thick rectangle of comforting pages. It was useless. All he could feel were rolls of dust, pebbles, and other lumps that were better left unguessed at. There had been a thunderstorm soon after the children had gone to bed that had soaked all the boys in the roofless fresh-air "cabin," and left them shivering in wet sleeping bags. But it wasn't the discomfort and the lack of reading matter that kept Harry awake. It was the thought of how feeble he had been that day. He had let them confiscate his books and his precious hat without a fight. His girl cousin had had the courage to stand up to these ghastly relatives, while he had remained timidly silent. He thought now of all the brave and scornful things he should have said. It seemed to Harry hideously probable that he was not made of the stuff the army would ever want.

Ames Oakes the Fifth was sniffling next to him.

"Are you crying about missing supper?" asked Harry cautiously. They had been warned that dire punishment awaited children who talked in their cabins at night.

"I'm not crying," lied Ames. "But I can't sleep. They took my Nice-and-Cosy away. That's my blanket, and I can't sleep without holding it and feeling the slidey edge between my fingers. I'm afraid."

"Afraid of what?" asked Harry, glad to take his mind off his own troubles.

"Lots of things: thunder and lightning, Coralene, those wolves, Danger. And I'm afraid that if I don't keep watch, something will fall out of the sky and flatten us. I always had a roof to protect me before."

"I wouldn't worry. The chances must be a million to one against that happening," reassured Harry.

"What if the earth started to spin faster and faster, until there was nothing to stop us from flying out into space?"

"Look," said Harry. "When I feel scared like that, I have some magic words to make things better. I usually keep them a secret, but I'll tell you a few if you like."

"Yes, please. The Sharkes make me feel that I'm the jellyfish and they are the—well—sharks."

"Next time you see them, try saying Omsk and Tomsk. And if you want to feel quite cheerful and sort of adventurous, repeat Timbuktu to yourself. I'll tell you some more later."

"Omsk and Tomsk, Tomsk 'n Omsk," said Ames.

61

"Timbuktu, Timbuktu, Timbuktu. Thanks, Harry. I think it's working, but I feel awfully hungry all the same. Have you got a word that makes you feel full?"

"No, but I'll tell you something else to say," offered Harry, thinking he might have let himself in for more geography than he had bargained for. "*The Sharkes are fishy.*"

Ames chortled. "The Sharkes are fishy," he repeated in delight. "That's lots better."

"Are the meals always as bad as tonight's?" asked Harry, thinking it impossible.

"That was better than most. You just wait till breakfast," warned a small voice.

"Listen," said Harry. "I'm going to get something for us to eat. I have an apricot bar and some other stuff in my backpack. I don't see why those Sharkes have the right to lock it away. Besides, I want my hat back, too."

Ames sat bolt upright in excitement. Then he sank back again as he remembered where Harry's pack was bound to be.

"It's no use. Miss Sharke always locks both the closet and the cabin, and wears all the keys on that string around her neck. Besides, Danger is let off her chain at night, to protect us from the wolves and the bears. She would eat you alive."

"I'd like to see her try," said Harry stoutly.

There was no retreat now that Ames was watching him with wide, admiring eyes. Harry said "Schleswig-Holstein" to himself, and wriggled out of his soggy sleeping bag.

Ames watched him run, crouching, from patch to patch of cover, like a soldier in *The Longest Day*.

"At least this is better than lying awake thinking what a coward I am," reflected Harry, feeling his stomach churn with excitement and terror.

Diana-Discipline's reception cabin was padlocked with a chain looped twice around the newly reinforced door frame. With an effort Harry found that he could make the rotting door jamb move, but he was not strong enough to budge it sufficiently to slip inside. There seemed nothing for it but to try and find a way of getting the keys from the Sharkes.

Concentrating on his hat and his stolen books, to avoid thinking of the probable consequences if he were to be caught, Harry squirmed, in best commando fashion, to the spot where the Sharkes' cabin light streamed through a knothole near the ground. Trusting that the child-eating dog was safely locked up, he put his eye to the hole, wishing Laura could witness his daring. He felt it quite made up for the poor showing he had made so far at Camp Nish Na Bosh Na.

13

Coralene Sharke was toasting pink marshmallows at a roaring fire. Thoughts of energy conservation and the importance of a balanced, sugar-free diet did not seem to be bothering her. As Harry watched, she stuffed five melting lumps into her mouth at once and opened another packet.

"The shopping up here is atrocious," she grumbled with bulging cheeks. "You would swear the butcher in Basswood had never heard of lobster, nor of lamb chops. As for chocolate-covered peanuts, they can't be got for love nor money."

"Those T-bone steaks were rather tough tonight," Egbert confirmed.

Diana-Discipline tossed a piece of candy to Danger, who caught it in midair. Her brother was doing something at the table, and as Coralene settled down to toast her second batch of marshmallows, Harry could see what it was.

Egbert Sharke, armed with an enormous eraser,

was working his way through a pile of postcards. "Gwen Jones says, 'Why don't you come and get me? It's even worse than I wrote before.' Such ingratitude! Diana," he said as he rubbed the side clean, "better give dear Gwen twenty extra pushups each morning. Isn't she that tall, dark girl?

"Well, well," he chuckled as he looked at the next one. "Young Benjamin has a clever notion. 'It is so great here with the kind Sharkes that you must come and see it immediately.' 'Come' and 'immediately' underlined three times. The first part will do very nicely. I only have to remove those last eight words. How kind of Ben to save me trouble.

"Dear me, here is a short one. It merely says 'Help.' Ah yes, I see it's from Ames Oakes the Fifth. I think I might try giving little Oakes remedial writing, if that's all he can manage in three minutes.

"Now here's one in care of the Opera House, Vienna. 'Am leaving for home tomorrow.' What a joke! That must be the new girl, our brand-new cousin Laura, who kindly supplied us with a list of addresses. I don't think having the Lewis pair turning up matters after all, since they've never met their lovable old Great-Aunt Adelaide."

Diana-Discipline guffawed.

Coralene said thoughtfully, "I think I had better tell Laura my poisonous-snake story. Otherwise she might try to make off through the woods. She looks to be a determined sort of girl."

Egbert busily rubbed out five more messages. "Now here is an interesting one. Melanie Paprika says, 'I love it here.' Is she the daughter of the mad Hungarian?''

"Give it to me." Coralene held the postcard to the fire. "You can never tell what tricks children think up. No, it doesn't seem to have a message in invisible ink. She must be going mad, too. Diana, give Melanie a morning in bed or a ten-mile jog, whichever seems to fit the case. Egbert, do hurry up. You're taking all night, and we must get our beauty sleep." She glanced in the mirror and patted her curls.

"You certainly need it," said her brother, smirking.

Coralene ignored the interruption. "All you have to do is erase the messages and write 'Camp is wonderful. Send more money,'" she said. "Surely you can do that without spending the whole evening on it? You used to be pretty swift at forgery, but if that last little stretch behind bars destroyed your nerve, then for heaven's sake just print. The parents won't notice. I must say the dollars are flowing in nicely, my dears. We were right to spend the first month milking the parents for all the small change we could. They've been most obliging. There should be plenty to buy the boat and other stuff we'll need later on for the serious part of the plan."

Diana-Discipline had finished her breathing exercises and was now standing upside down against the wall, to encourage the flow of blood to the brain. "If you ask me, I think I should leave the Lewis boy alone," she said. "No telling where a card to that Washington address might end up. CIA files, I shouldn't be surprised."

66

Egbert shuddered and used three tissues in rapid succession. He tossed Harry's postcard on the fire.

Diana yawned and turned right way up again. "This was a wonderful idea of yours, Coral Bells," she said. "I am having a delightful summer."

"Don't call me Coral Bells," snapped her sister.

"Well, I don't find it delightful. In fact, I can't wait to get out of this dump," said Egbert, sneezing.

"Poor Snuffles," said Diana-Discipline.

"Don't ever let me hear you say that again," snarled her brother. "Coralene, it's high time we moved on to the second part of your plan. I can't stand both my sisters and the fresh air much longer."

"And we," she replied, "certainly can't stand an overdose of our dearest brother."

Harry felt a tug on his sweat shirt and turned around to find Ames.

"All the others went to sleep and I got scared again. So I said 'Omskytomsk,' and came to find you," Ames said. "Couldn't we get into the bus and drive it away while they're in there?"

The beautiful simplicity of this plan took Harry's breath away. Inside the cabin, Danger sniffed and shifted uneasily.

"Give her another marshmallow," commanded her owner.

Harry decided it was high time to move. Ames didn't have much of an idea of how to keep quiet.

"Okay," he whispered. "Let's try."

"I sometimes drive my father's golf cart," Ames whispered loudly.

"Shh."

The bus was unlocked, but there were no keys in the ignition, nor above the sun visor. Harry didn't know where else to look, and in fact was not altogether sorry that he wasn't required to make a dash for freedom in the VW bus, since he had no idea how to drive. So as not to be totally defeated, he took Egbert's stack of chocolate bars, which were balanced on an outsize box of Kleenex, and stuffed the small paper bag beside them into his pocket as well, in hopes that its contents were edible.

The moon went behind a cloud, and Danger began to bark furiously. Harry and Ames scurried back to their roofless quarters just in the nick of time. Egbert came out into the night complaining, "If one of you little brats is stirring, by golly, I'll have your guts for garters. I'll . . . I'll feed you to Danger for breakfast."

"You were brave," said Ames in open admiration as they munched a chocolate bar each, keeping the rest for future emergencies. "And this is the best chocolate I've ever tasted. Do you think I should ask my father to buy the factory?"

"Start by asking for a couple of bars," advised Harry. The kid obviously had a wild imagination.

"Harry," he said sleepily a little later, "would you call me Acorn? That's what I'm called at home, and I don't feel like the same me when people say Oakes or Ames."

"Sure, Acorn," agreed Harry, who was feeling that he might make a hero of the Resistance after all.

14

Breakfast, like all meals at Camp Nish Na Bosh Na, was announced by a sharp blast on Diana-Discipline's whistle. Laura was hungry enough to scramble from her bunk and run to line up with the others. There were some advantages in not being able to wash, dress, or comb one's hair. It gave getting up a certain speed and simplicity.

The meal consisted of lukewarm, lumpy porridge, doled out of a large iron pan by D-Discipline. One scoop each. "A healthy diet is free of animal fats," she said to Laura, who was looking around hopefully for some milk, or bread and butter. "Try some lake water."

Ten minutes later, another whistle sent the children scurrying to their places in the next line. This time they were lined up by height. Diana-D marched alongside, consulting a list.

The smallest four were sent to clean out Coralene's cabin. The next were sent to roof repairs, the next to working on the dock, the next to pulling weeds, and so on down the line. Laura noted that Harry and Acorn, who stood on tiptoe next to him, were assigned to road building. She hoped that last night's threat would be forgotten, but there was no such luck. Gwen, sagging at the knees, and Laura, stretching in order to stand next to her, were sent to sort a load of spoiled spinach that Egbert had secured in a deal with the Basswood sanitation department. The slimy leaves went into the pot for soup. The crisp ones were saved for future delights.

"Usually kitchen duty is best, because you get to scrape the pots and eat the stuff sticking to the bottom," said Gwen out of the side of her mouth, in best Nish Na Bosh Na fashion.

Laura made a grimace at the congealed porridge. She would have to be even hungrier than she was now to eat that stuff. A vision of thick, buttery toast, smothered in honey, danced through her mind.

"Laura," she said sternly to herself. "Don't think about toast. Just find a way to get us out of here." She wondered if Harry's work would be near enough the main road for him to slip away, stop a passing car, and explain their plight.

Harry had been hoping the same thing, but to his disappointment he found that the Sharkes were taking no chances. The road repairs had not progressed above a mile from the camp. The children were expected to uproot weeds, young trees, and general vegetation from the track, and then level it by shoveling dirt from the center of the road into the ruts.

"I regard this as one of the New Games," said Diana-Discipline, leaving them to their duties.

At noon, Diana-Discipline inspected the kitchen. "Waste not, want not," she said, stirring the soup with satisfaction. "There is no further need for you here. Only adults eat lunch at Nish Na Bosh Na. We have to reduce puppy fat and get you all in trim for some Olympic-style canoeing. Go and help the road builders."

Walking along the track with Gwen to join the road crew, Laura cheered up. The woods smelled wonderfully of resin, and there was a stillness, an absence of any sound of cars or indeed of humans (except for the distant shrilling of Diana-Discipline's whistle). This fascinated Laura. She was used to a constant background noise of city traffic. It was amazing to hear nothing but their feet swishing through the long grass and the odd chirp and squeak from a midday bird or a surprised squirrel. It was only as she realized how far they were from any possibility of rescue that the sounds of silence began to appall Laura. She greeted Harry with enthusiasm. You certainly valued friends in a place like Camp Nish Na Bosh Na.

By midafternoon the road crew was tired. Laura, who was not used to this kind of work, was longing for a rest and suggested that they had all done enough not to get into serious trouble if they took a break. The others agreed readily. So they posted a lookout, flung themselves down on a patch of grass, and watched the sunlight slant through the aspen leaves and dapple the peeling bark of the paper birches and the dark trunks of the spruce.

"The Sharkes are fishy," announced Acorn, and rolled on the ground howling with laughter.

The others joined in, laughing at Acorn as much as anything else. They realized, with a lifting of their spirits, that out there in the woods, no one could hear you and you didn't have to talk out of the side of your mouth.

"Our name is *Jawse*, with an *e* of course," said one girl in an imitation of Coralene's refined tones.

They all laughed until they hurt.

"Knock, knock," said a boy who had not so far said a word.

"Who's there?"

"Egbert."

"Egbert who?"

"Egbert no bacon."

They all rolled over, hugging themselves with hysterical laughter again.

Harry tried: "What happened to the Tower of Pisa?"

"What?"

"Cora leaned on it."

As jokes go, it wasn't much, but the response was gratifying. The entire road crew flung themselves around on the grass in new delight. "Cora leaned," crowed Acorn. "Coralened. Get it?"

"We get it, Acorn," said Gwen.

"It's all right for all of you. Coralene isn't your aunt," said Laura, sighing.

"I don't believe she's yours either. There must be some mistake," said Gwen loyally. "Oh dear, if I wasn't so hungry, this afternoon would be great. It's the first nice thing that's happened since we got here."

Harry felt in his pocket and produced two chocolate bars, which with heroic self-denial he had saved to share with Laura and the others. He was rewarded by the respect with which they all looked at him.

"However did you prevent them taking it away from you?" asked a boy named Wade. "They even took my last half-stick of gum."

"Oh, I didn't bring it with me. Acorn and I stole it from the bus last night," said Harry, with a fine show of nonchalance.

"You didn't!" breathed Laura. "However could you risk your life with Danger?"

Harry tried to look modest. He was satisfied that he had impressed his capable cousin with his cool and daring.

"Did you get anything else?" asked Laura hopefully.

"Just these," said Harry, bringing out the paper bag. "I don't really know what they are. They're some sort of dried seeds with a nice smell, but they aren't much to eat."

Laura took a pinch, sniffed, bit one, and sniffed again. "It's anise seed," she said. She wasn't chief cook in the Lewis household for nothing. "I wonder why Egbert would have that in the bus. I can't exactly see any of the Sharkes baking cookies," she added.

"I know why," said Acorn unexpectedly. "Treats for Danger."

They looked at him blankly. He explained, "Dogs love the taste of anise, so you let them have a little as a special treat. My dad owns a circus, and they train the animals that way. When they learn a new trick, they get an extra lick. I expect the elephants get a whole bucket."

They all looked at the little boy doubtfully. Acorn must have been making it up.

"The trouble with chocolate is that it just whets your appetite for more," said a quiet girl called Jane, who had looked around vaguely ever since Diana-Discipline had locked away her spectacles.

"You're right," said Laura. "I'm going to explore a little. Perhaps we can find some berries to eat, or birds' eggs, or roots, or something," she added a little vaguely. She wasn't sure what a Minnesota forest yielded in the way of edibles.

"Oh Laura, don't," begged Gwen. "These woods are full of wild animals, and if they bite you, then you'll die horribly."

"How do you know?" demanded Laura. "I bet Coralene just made that up to frighten us into staying in her prison. Harry's book proved that the wolves were a lie."

She marched firmly into the undergrowth. If her bookworm cousin could be brave, then she had to keep her end up, too.

"Laura," she said to herself. "Forward, my girl.

We are not scared in broad daylight." She pushed through some bushes into a clearing.

In a few minutes, Laura was back with some wild strawberries in her hand. The road crew, forgetting their fears of rabid skunks, and the need for a lookout, followed her eagerly. A little way beyond the dense part of the forest, the trees opened out into a large, sandy hollow. Laura pointed to a slope that was covered by a mat of ripe, wild strawberries. With a cheer, the children set to and ate ravenously.

Gwen thoughtfully stowed some away for her cabinmates. Now that she had overcome her Sharke-induced fears, Gwen proved surprisingly knowledge-able about the woods. "I saw a place like this in Wisconsin, when I used to visit my grandmother. It must be an old gravel pit where they dug the foundations for the camp or the road. They always fill up first with flowers and bushes. Then little cottonwoods and aspens and birches grow for a while before the forest takes over again. This is a teaberry plant," she said, tasting a leaf. "I think that is wintergreen," she added, pointing out a small bush just inside the forest proper. "You can eat the leaves."

They were all chewing the teaberry and winter-green busily, and the cold porridge had faded to a bad dream, when they heard a sound as unexpected as it was welcome. A car was coming. Cheering jubi-lantly, the children ran back to the road and stood waving wildly to stop the majestic green Chrysler Imperial driving toward them.

Inside the car, Mr. James Dubious and his wife looked with some alarm at the strangely dressed children jumping up and down in the road.

"I don't think you should stop, Pootsie. It's not as if they were normal children. Who knows what they might do?" said Mrs. Dubious, clutching her purse as if she suspected an ambush by bandits.

"Just what I was thinking, Tootsie," said her husband, treading on the accelerator. "I think we should ask Mrs. Sharke how you handle disturbed kids. You don't want to interrupt their therapy, or whatever it is."

"I declare," said Mrs. Dubious, when they were safely past, "they do look a wild and dangerous bunch. I hope Mrs. Sharke has enough keepers, or whatever it is they call them. Drive a little faster, honey. One of them is trying to run behind, and is waving in a truly lunatic fashion."

15

"We have enjoyed our little chat," purred Coralene.
"One does so miss civilized company in these backwoods. We mean, only in this teeny-weeny distant
corner of your magnificent state," she corrected, as
she saw a frown crease Mr. Dubious's pink forehead.
"But my sister is trying to help those poor, confused
youngsters, and where dear Diana-Discipline goes,
Egbert and I follow. Family loyalty, you know."

"Blood runs thicker than water," interposed dear
Diana-D herself, in a faintly alarming fashion.

"Indeed I know, indeed, indeed. I can't tell you
how much I admire your wonderful work here,"
responded Mr. Dubious, with a hundred-watt sincere look.

"My stars, yes," echoed his wife. "When I saw
how crazy those kids on the road acted, my first
thought was what a grand job you all were doing, to
give the poor things a summer in the open air."

Coralene simpered sweetly and changed the subject. "How becoming that dress is, my dear. Did you purchase it in Paris?"

"Land sakes, no," said Mrs. Dubious. "I saw it in the Sears catalogue. But speaking of clothes, Mrs. Sharke, what unusual ones your campers wear."

"Yes," said Coralene smoothly. "How alert of you to notice. It's one of our little experiments here, and quite the success."

"It's democratic," added Egbert. "Puts everyone on an equal footing—flat. Just like some Olympic hopefuls, eh, Diana?"

"Perhaps we Republicans should try it," murmured Mrs. Dubious uncertainly.

"By the way," said Mr. Dubious, rubbing his pudgy hands together, "perhaps I should mention that it is almost impossible to find this place. Only this morning I met some parents, Mr. and Mrs. Ames Oakes the Fourth, who said they had been driving around for hours, trying to follow some map you supplied. I gather they had to leave for an urgent appointment in New York, but were planning to return later in the week and ask the Basswood police for guidance. Mrs. Oakes was most anxious for young Ames to have an extra sweater. It seems he has never left home before, and she was afraid he might catch cold. Mr. Oakes wanted to interview the young man on money management. He has apparently been sending twice-weekly requests for more cash. Of course, I didn't feel it appropriate to butt in and give them directions until I had discovered your wishes, my dear Mrs. Coralene." Mr. Dubious smiled his most oily smile.

"That's torn it," said Diana-Discipline.

"Yes, I rather thought you would want to know a parent was on the track, so to speak," said Mr. Dubious, shooting a shrewd glance at the tumble-down buildings.

"I am sure our guests will excuse you, sister, if you need to get back to your little charges," said Coralene coldly.

"What? Oh yes. Well, toodle-oo," said Diana-Discipline, and loped back to the lakeside to supervise the dock-building.

"What a noble soul," sighed Mrs. Dubious.

Egbert snorted.

"What dear Diana meant just now," explained Coralene, "is that little Oakes is one of our bad cases. A visit from his parents would be the worst possible thing for him at this stage. He would be sure to have a relapse."

"How tragic." Mrs. Dubious shook her head sadly.

"I think we understand each other," Mr. Dubious was saying, leaning confidentially toward Coralene. "When I sold you this property in March for a modest price . . ."

"For a price that was daylight robbery," corrected Coralene.

"Well, as I was saying, the price was low in view of a few little problems."

"Such as the lake acting as the sewage dump for some crummy town," said Egbert.

"Precisely. Well, it seems that the State Health Agency has just ruled that Minor Falls must build a proper waste-disposal system. With the lake cleaned up, this becomes a very interesting piece of land—a bargain, in fact, Mrs. Sharke. What business acumen you have in that pretty head of yours."

Egbert looked so interested that he forgot to blow his nose. A large drip hung from the end. Coralene tossed her sausage curls and recrossed her legs, so that she could admire the way her turquoise toenails vibrated against her purple wedgies.

Mr. Dubious continued. "Now I suggest you sell this land back to me this fall, when you retire from the camping business. I assume you intend to leave at the end of this summer. A second season might present real problems, to say nothing of reduced profits."

"Surely," protested Coralene, "you realize that we are not in this for the money, although it is worth every cent we spend to see the smiles return to the children's lips and the roses to their cheeks."

"Quite, quite," said Mr. Dubious impatiently. "But unless we come to an understanding, my dear Coralene, I shall feel impelled to give directions to the camp to any parents I might meet. I had also thought of speaking to the girl at the *Northern Light* in Basswood. I hear she's eager to make a name for herself as a fearless investigative reporter, and I have no doubt that she could make an arresting front-page story about your unusual living conditions."

Egbert winced at the word *arresting*. Mr. Dubious

warmed to his subject. "I don't doubt that the local TV station would want a film, too. Some things look highly photogenic here."

"How exciting. You would be a celebrity, Mrs. Sharke," cried Mrs. Dubious.

Mrs. Sharke did not look overjoyed at the prospect. Egbert looked positively jumpy. "Since peace and quiet are so important to the children, Mr. Dubious," Coralene said icily, "I would appreciate your efforts to ensure an undisturbed summer. If no parent manages to find us, we would give you first option to buy this charming piece of real estate. But you must realize that its value has gone up enormously, what with the new possibilities you mention, and our own road repairs, new dock, and other improvements."

"Gee, this camp story could be such headline stuff that once it breaks I expect the major TV networks will pick it up," mused Mr. Dubious, "and broadcast interviews with the three of you, nationwide. Fifteen thousand, and not a wooden nickel more, is my offer. Generous, under the circumstances."

"If you say so, Mr. Dubious," said Coralene, grinding her teeth. "Since you insist, we will sell Camp Nish Na Bosh Na back to you this fall for that paltry amount, so long as we can rely on your silence until then."

"I do wish we could stay for supper," said Mrs. Dubious, leading the way out. "This fresh air has given me such an appetite, and I am sure Miss Diana is quite the chef. Unfortunately, we must get back before dark, and your road is so tricky, isn't it?"

81

Mr. Dubious turned his car around, flattening some young balsam trees in the process.

Mrs. Dubious leaned out to say "What a lovely doggie," before rolling her window up tightly and locking the door. "Honey, drive fast past those crazy kids. Why, this afternoon I even thought one was going to jump right onto the car, and there's no telling what they might try this time."

"Okay, Tootsie." Mr. Dubious tossed a piece of birch bark off his seat, with a casual glance at the S.O.S. scratched on it. "Let's go and drink to huge profits and quick returns. I think this afternoon was well worth the drive. If only that stubborn old Adelaide Lewis was half so easy to persuade."

Coralene stormed down to the lake. "Interfering busybodies. Crook! Thief! Blackmailer! May his condominiums collapse in a million splinters. I hope another Ice Age covers this God-forsaken land. Parents, too! What right do parents have to come snooping? Diana," she snapped, "get the brats fed and in bed by six. We have to discuss the second stage of our plan urgently."

"Atta-girl," said Diana-Discipline, giving a mighty blast on her whistle.

"Spinach up!"

16

The dinner whistle surprised the children, who had only just thrown themselves down on their bunks. Laura and Gwen's cabinmates shot out of the door like rabbits who hear the footfall of a beagle, or, as Diana-Discipline would have preferred to put it, like Olympic-prospect sprinters.

"I'm not going to taste a drop of that spinach gunge," vowed Laura.

"By the time you've spent two weeks dining in the North Woods with the Sharkes, you'll eat anything," promised Gwen glumly.

Laura wished she could cheer her up; Gwen was always so kind and helpful, both to Laura herself and to all the smaller children. There wasn't much to joke about at Nish Na Bosh Na, however. She decided that the best thing she could do for Gwen was to organize their escape from this dreadful place.

Farther down the lake path, in the fresh-air cabin, Acorn was fast asleep. Harry tried to shake him awake. "Come on, Acorn," he said urgently, "or we'll both miss dinner."

Acorn groaned. "No, not already. I'm tired right through, from one corner to the other."

He turned over. Harry shook him more roughly. "You can't miss dinner again. You'll be nothing but skin and bones."

Reluctantly, Acorn opened one eye. Then the full meaning of Harry's words hit him, and both boys ran like hares for the dinner line.

Diana-Discipline was ladling out the spinach soup, which contained mushrooms found in the woods earlier in the day. "They look edible to me," she had said. "Of course I'm no expert, but we'll find out by morning if there were some wrong 'uns among them. Ha, ha, ha! What?"

Two campers who were toadying up in the hope of gaining privileges laughed mechanically. Everyone else was silent. There was chicken in the soup, which all the children except Gwen thought incredible luck. Gwen had spent part of the morning emptying chicken packages into the pot. They had all been clearly marked "Eat by April 1st." Today must be the last day of June, she reckoned.

"Oops. Two losers tonight. Pity to miss such a nourishing, iron-rich treat," said Diana-Discipline as the last dollop of green sludge fell into the bowl ahead of Harry's. "Unlucky again, Ames," she said. "That's not the way to get selected for the Olympics. When will you learn to get a move on?"

The little boy turned away, tears trickling down

his face despite a brave effort to keep them back by blinking very fast.

Laura could stand no more. "Here," she said, handing her bowl to Acorn, "have this. I wasn't going to eat it anyway."

With that, she marched up to Diana-Discipline, and, in her outrage at the injustice, did something that none of the other campers at Nish Na Bosh Na would have done save in their wildest dreams.

"You ought to be ashamed of yourself, Miss Sharke," she stormed. "Bullying defenseless children, inventing cruel rules, giving us this horrible stuff to eat and not even having enough of it to go around."

Laura surprised even herself by the words that came tumbling out. There was no going back now. "Laura, my girl," she said to herself, using a phrase she didn't even know she knew, "you might as well be hung for a sheep as a lamb."

To Diana-Discipline's face, which was slowly turning purple with rage, she said, "You should share the food that goes into your sister's cabin. Our parents have paid for it. Don't think we kids are ignorant of your midnight feasts."

The children stared wide-eyed, half admiring Laura and half dreading the tornado of wrath she had surely provoked. Laura dug her fingernails into the palms of her hands so that the pain would give her something to think about besides Miss Sharke, who drew herself up to her full six foot three inches, puffed her chest out like a bullfrog, and bellowed at Laura in a voice the girl thought might be heard in Basswood

85

and would, with luck, send the fire engine to their aid.

"Outrageous nerve! How dare you take that tone with me? How, how dare you be impudent to someone who was nearly selected for the Tokyo Olympics? A night in the cooler shall teach you manners, my girl."

She put a fearsome hand on the back of Laura's neck and marched her away, throwing a threat over her shoulder that the first child to speak would be thrown in the lake.

When they reached the closet where the packs had been thrown, Diana-Discipline selected a key from the bunch around her neck, opened the door, and threw Laura in.

17

As Diana-Discipline's furious footsteps receded, Laura felt around in the dark through the pile of purloined campers' possessions, and eventually located her knife. Just having the familiar heft of it in her hand made her feel better. It was a bright red Swiss army knife with a loop at one end to hang from her belt. Her thumb felt for the small roughness that was the white Swiss cross in its shield.

"This is against my better judgment," her mother had said when she gave it to her on her tenth birthday. "But since you want it so badly, and since it does seem just the knife for a practical character like you . . ."

Laura remembered how the knife had rolled into her hand from the last fold of wrapping paper, as if it belonged there, and how surprised she had been at its weight that first time. The knife had rarely left her pocket from then until she encountered her hateful relatives and their "arrival ceremony."

Laura thought of the food in Harry's pack and continued her private version of blindman's buff. Her fingers found the satin ribbon of Acorn's blanket, and then Harry's army cap. It had been her father's, so she put it on. It gave her a surge of courage. With that and the knife, she should certainly be able to outwit the Sharkes and escape from this so-called camp. For good measure, she tried Harry's method for feeling brave. "Omsk and Tomsk. Detroit and Cleveland," she muttered. Laura began to rehearse the noble speech she would make when the key turned in the door and she faced Diana-Discipline's wrath once more.

"I am not in the least sorry," she would say. "You needn't think you are going to make me apologize. I shall never do so, even if I have to stay here forever. You were bullying and starving a defenseless little boy."

A vision of Miss Sharke's purple face swam into her mind.

"Schleswig-Holstein," she muttered hastily. It was like putting armor on. "Chimborazo." What other strange places could she think of?

"I am going to march straight out of this awful place and never, never return. I shall tell the police about conditions here," she said to an imaginary Coralene, who cried, "Oh Laura, my sweet child, please, please don't do that. It's all been such a mistake and I am so sorry. Here's the telephone."

Laura's fingers closed on the lumps of dried food Harry had bought in Basswood, what seemed an age ago. She blessed his extravagance now, as she gnawed a knob of dried carrot and stuffed the spaghetti dinner and other packets into her pockets.

The door of the cabin opened. Laura stopped chewing. The noise her jaws had been making sounded deafening, and her brave desire to tell her captors what she thought of them leaked out of the soles of her sneakers. She tweaked the peak of her cap, and regained enough courage to chew her dried carrot very, very softly.

"Now, Egbert, get a move on," said Coralene, noticeably less sweetly than usual. "You have the addresses? Wherever did Diana put the photographs and the locks of hair?"

"In the big closet with the luggage, I suppose," answered her brother.

Laura's stomach looped the loop.

"No, here they are on this shelf. How careless of her not to lock them up. A photo and a lock of hair goes to each parent, along with the ransom note."

Laura peeped through a crack. Egbert Sharke was addressing envelopes and swiftly tossing them over to his sister. She selected a photograph and a lock of hair from the pile on the shelf before her, to go into each envelope.

"I do wish Diana would get here. She's taking forever to get those brats into bed. It's already six o'clock, and I can't tell if this hair belongs to Debbie Adams or Beth Bowles."

"Does this sound right to you?" asked Egbert, scribbling on a yellow legal pad. "Make that illegal pad," thought Laura. "'Send ten thousand dollars or you will never see this child again.' You don't think we should make it a hundred thousand, do you?"

"Don't be greedy, Egbert," Coralene said in a snaky tone. "Trust you to want to kill the goose that lays the golden eggs. Besides, that's far too abrupt. A little politeness never comes amiss. Don't forget, summer camps are superior affairs. And we need some threats, so the parents don't delay in producing the money. Take this down."

She started to dictate: *"Your child needs ten thousand dollars for unexpected camping expenses. Await instructions on where to deliver the money in unmarked twenty-dollar bills. We enclose a lock of your child's hair as a reminder that we will be compelled to undertake brain surgery if the money is not forthcoming. If you go to the police, rest assured that the enclosed photograph is the last you will see of your offspring. As you can see, your little darling does not look happy. You can restore a smile to this face by prompt payment.*

"Sign it, 'a well-wisher.' What a pity I am the only member of the family with a creative imagination." Coralene sighed and consulted a list from her heliotrope purse. "You're going to have to drive into Basswood first thing tomorrow to mail these and stock up on supplies for the journey. I've already contacted the grocery stores. They can let us have quantities of overripe apples and bananas at most advantageous prices. Black bananas are good enough for children. Get thirty pounds of liver. It's on sale this week. The man told me he wanted to clear out some sacks of turnips that had been around for the best part of a year. Take the lot. Tell him we need them for craft projects, and you may get a reduced rate. By the way, I think porterhouse steak travels best. Be sure you get some juicy ones for the three of us.

"What a lot of work," she sighed. "If only that odious Mr. Dubious and his imbecile wife hadn't come snooping, we'd have had time to manage our departure from this place so much more comfortably. Go and find Diana. It's high time she was cooking our pork chops. And don't forget to let the dog out, Egbert. We can't have the kids wandering around. It would never do to mislay one of those little creeps at this stage."

They went out, leaving Laura frantic to escape. "Laura, we've got to get out and warn the others," she muttered to herself as she shook the door with all her might. The lock held firm.

"It's no use," she sighed near despair, swallowing some dried carrot that refused to be chewed. Then she touched the lucky hat, murmured "Vladivostok," and got to work with the strongest blade of her Swiss army pocketknife.

18

Harry lay in his sleeping bag, thinking of Laura's incredible bravery and hoping that, locked in her closet, she was not feeling the panic that clutched him whenever he was confined in small, enclosed spaces. He rolled a little closer to his fellow sufferers and whispered, "Hey, you guys, we've got to make a fight for freedom."

He caught sight of wide, appalled eyes above a couple of prison-surplus gray bags, and went on. "They can't hurt us if we all refuse to obey them and simply march out to the main road together."

Two of the bags rolled away from him as if he had measles. A third boy explained apologetically, in a low voice, "It's no good. I've thought of that. For one thing, they would hear of the plans. Some kids get extra food for telling them about any trouble in the camp. For another, everyone is too scared of being locked up in a closet, getting no meals, doing a hundred extra pushups, putting in more time peeling moldy potatoes, or any other of their rotten punishments, to risk it. You should have been here the first week. Some kids tried to rebel, and Coralene scared them into nightmares. Most of us decided then to wait it out until the end of the summer."

"Well, then," said Harry, "if you won't stand and face them, why don't we all just run away quietly?"

"Where to?" asked one of the boys. "My parents are getting a divorce. They sent me here until everything was settled. I don't know where I am to live anymore."

"My parents would never believe me if I told them about conditions here," explained another boy. "They would get mad at me for making things up."

"There are wolves and things in the woods. It'd be worse than Diana-D and her whistle," said a boy called Brett.

"And what about Danger?" asked his friend Sandy. "She would never let us get away. Ugh. I can almost feel her fangs in my legs now."

The boys all shivered.

"I'll come, Harry," whispered Acorn.

"Great kid," said Harry, wishing the volunteer had been someone older and more reliable. Acorn would be something of a handicap in the escape.

"Shall we steal the bus?" Acorn asked.

There was an audible gasp from all the boys in the open-air cabin, then a short silence while each camper entertained the entrancing notion of getting into the rainbow bus and driving far away from Camp Nish Na Bosh Na.

"No," said Harry. "We couldn't find the keys, Acorn. Remember? We'll have to go through the woods. Stay here while I get Laura. There must be some way of freeing her, and then the three of us will go."

A door slammed shut in the distance as Diana-Discipline finished her rounds and rejoined the other Sharkes. Holding the small paper bag tightly, Harry set out, devoutly hoping that Acorn had not been making up his story about dogs and anise seed.

Danger was sniffing her way along the lake path. She seemed twice as large by moonlight. Harry timidly whispered, "Here, Danger." Danger didn't seem to know her name. So Harry called a little louder. This time the dog lifted her head and looked as if she was going to bark, but changed her mind and padded over to investigate. Harry distinctly felt his heart jump into his throat as he held out a handful of anise seed. What if Laura was wrong in her identification of the seeds? He brushed away a tear at the thought of his parents weeping over his mangled corpse. The dog came nearer and stopped. The whole scene was so unlike anything Harry had ever been involved in that he wondered if it was real at all. Perhaps he was starring in a horror movie— *Beyond Jaws*? The thought of cameras rolling in the pine trees nerved him to crawl forward toward the monster, playing the brave captain who risks his life so his men can escape. Danger took one bound, and the next instant she was licking the seeds out of Harry's hand, wagging her tail, and looking up into his face with slavish devotion.

Unutterably relieved, Harry crept on toward Laura's prison. Danger, deciding this was a good game that might well involve more treats, trotted beside him. Every now and then she licked a bare ankle with a warm, affectionate tongue.

From the back of the cabin came the muffled rasping of Laura's carpentry. Putting his mouth to a gap between the floor and the wall, Harry called to her. The rasping stopped, and a moment later he caught the gleam of an eye in the crack.

"Harry, thank goodness," said Laura. "I was just beginning to think that nobody in the whole world cared where I was."

"Are you starving?" Harry asked sympathetically. "Look, I saved some bread from supper. It's rather hard, I'm afraid, but it doesn't have any of that green stuff on it."

"Thanks," said Laura, "eat it yourself. You missed supper, too, and I've been feasting on your dried food. I hope you don't mind. It was all here except the apricot bar, which Diana-D must have swiped. I've got your hat, by the way, and Acorn's blanket. My fingers are aching from trying to loosen these boards. Do you think you could have a go from your side?"

"Sure," said Harry. "Just hand me the knife."

"Try the pick blade," advised Laura. "It seems to dig into the rotten wood pretty well. I've got four nails out so far, and some are missing already."

They took turns handing the knife back and forth and loosening the board, while Laura told Harry what she had overheard.

"They're going to kidnap us and blackmail our parents. I couldn't believe it at first—the camp itself is bad enough—but I heard them say so with my own two ears not an hour ago."

"They've already done the kidnapping," replied Harry bitterly. "Dear Aunt Adelaide-Coralene and our charming step-cousins-in-law. To think I used to be proud of my family."

"No, it's worse than you think. They plan to take us away from here and hide us somewhere else, in case that fat man in the car comes back."

"That settles it," said Harry. "We have to escape as soon as possible."

"I've been thinking of a way," said Laura. "We'll get everyone to break out together. If we go in different directions they can't catch us all, and someone is sure to be able to reach help."

"Here, hand me that knife again," said Harry. "You're doing more than your share. No, that won't work. I've been talking to everyone in my cabin about escaping, but the Sharkes have scared them silly. They all plan simply to endure Nish Na Bosh Na until the end of the summer. The boys seem to be more afraid of the woods and all the nonsense our dear relatives have told them about the area than they are of the Ugly Sisters themselves."

"Not forgetting the Ugly Brother," said Laura, thinking it likely that Harry hadn't approached his cabinmates properly. "Never mind, if the boys are chicken the girls will manage it."

Harry was about to make a heated retort, when

they both heard the unmistakeable thud, thud, thud of Diana-Discipline jogging down the path. The children froze. Diana noisily fumbled with the key in the lock, and entered the cabin.

"Laura Lewis," she said, "I will unlock this closet when you tell me how truly sorry you are for your insolence. I am waiting. Begin."

There was a long silence, in which Harry's heart seemed to be booming audibly.

"Well, Laura?"

Silence.

"Obstinate girl! You don't want to force me to keep you in this place all night, do you?"

Laura's voice came, small but frigidly polite. "You may leave me in the closet if you wish, Miss Sharke, but you cannot alter the truth. You are a cruel and unjust woman."

Harry resolved to give the lieutenant's hat to Laura. She was worthy of it.

"We shall see about that, Miss High and Mighty," said Diana-Discipline. "I assure you, wretched child, that you have no idea how cruel I can be. For starters, I will leave you here all night. No apology, no release and no food."

Diana-Discipline locked the door and pounded up the path, fury making her even noisier and more vigorous than usual.

Shaken by her wrath, both children silently turned their attention to working the loosened board back and forth. Finally it came free. Laura flattened herself on the floor and wriggled her head out, but, to her

97

bitter disappointment, the rest of her was securely wedged inside. She lay on her back for a moment, breathing the fresh air and listening to the comforting rustle of the birches. A waft of less fragrant air came from the water, but the stars were out over the little lake, and suddenly she felt equal to anything. The next moment, she nearly woke the whole camp up with a scream of alarm, as a rough tongue began to lick her ear.

"It's only Danger," Harry reassured.

Despite Harry's amazing cool, Laura did not find this news particularly calming. Harry gave the dog another lick of anise seed, and Laura could hear a tail thumping with gratitude and delight as Harry explained his technique for taming wild animals.

Laura handed out the precious hat, what was left of the dried food, and Acorn's Nice-and-Cosy. Harry badly wanted a book but decided that escaping came first, so he tied Acorn's tattered treasure around his waist and cached the other things, while Laura took the knife and returned to the wearisome task of removing another board so she could get free of her closet prison. Before she had finally managed it, a flashlight announced that Diana-Discipline had returned and put an end to Harry and Laura's plans for an escape that night.

"My sister and I have decided to make an example of you to the whole camp," she announced through the locked door.

Laura hastily slipped the knife into a pocket and started piling backpacks over the gap she had made.

Diana-Discipline unlocked the door, but was too intent on what she held in her hands to notice what Laura had been up to.

"Tonight you will go back to your cabin wearing this. Don't think for a moment that you can take it off; I shall check on you from time to time. It will be your camp uniform for the rest of your stay with us, cousin."

She knotted around Laura's shoulders a placard that read, DO NOT SPEAK TO ME. I WAS RUDE TO THE KIND SHARKES.

19

Next morning, Egbert returned from his daily trip to
the post office with a load of canoes strapped to the
top of the bus. The children looked up from replacing
rotten roof beams, building the dock, leveling the
lake front, and hauling sand for a beach.

"Perhaps it's going to be a real camp at last," said
one of the youngest, wistfully.

"With them in control?" said a wiser boy. "Nuts."

Coralene herself, tying on a mauve nylon net headscarf, came out to supervise getting the canoes into
the water.

"It's the wig," explained Gwen to Laura. "She has
to do that to keep it from blowing off."

"There must be a letter for me. My mother promised
to write every day," said one bold child, eyeing the
fat bundle of mail in Egbert's hand.

"Not a thing. Tough luck, kiddo," he replied blandly,
and retired to his cabin sneezing.

"Good riddance," said Harry, squinting at the words

stamped on the boats he was unloading: REJECTED AS UNFIT FOR USE. MINNESOTA PARKS RECREATION BOAT INSPECTION DEPT.

He pointed it out silently to Laura.

"I'll collect the girls to escape with us," she muttered.

"Come here, boy," shouted Diana-Discipline. "Help load these canoes with provisions. On the double. We haven't got all day." She swatted at some large black stinging flies, which were a feature of the Nish Na Bosh Na waterfront. "Take two loads at once. We have to build those muscles."

Harry staggered down to the lake with a sack of rotten turnips under one arm and a sack of powdered skim milk, originally destined for the Korean War, under the other. The children formed a chain and handed down twenty five-pound tins of artificial mashed potatoes, fifteen sacks of dried dog food (fish flavor), and more tins of Doggie's Yum-Yum Stew than Danger could ever eat, although she was three times as well fed as the children.

Laura moved up to the girl loading next to her. The placard thumped unpleasantly with each step she took. "Hey, Beth," she said, out of the side of her mouth. "Do you want to get out of this place?"

"Are you kidding?" replied Beth.

"Then get behind my canoe. We'll make a break for it."

"Thanks, but I daren't. That dog will track you down and surely kill you. I'd rather put up with D-Discipline's food a bit longer."

"We can take care of the dog," said Laura. But Beth had already moved away from her dangerous companion. Laura ducked behind a canoe.

"Psst, Judy," she said.

"Shh. Go away. That placard says I mustn't talk to you."

"Say, Cindy," said Laura, under cover of an armload of paddles, "we're going to escape. Follow my canoe when I give the signal."

"Thanks, but I couldn't face those woods, with the angry Indians, and snakes, and rabid wolves and things." Cindy too put some hasty distance between herself and this troublemaker.

"I don't think I could," said Jane. "Without my glasses I can't see a thing. What's that you're wearing on your chest?"

"No way. She'll murder you," said Amy.

"Gee, things can't get worse here, so they're bound to get better. I guess I'll stay," said Marcie.

By the end of the loading, Laura had discovered that Gwen was the only girl prepared to try to escape with her.

"I was wrong. The girls won't come either," she told Harry. "Talk about a feeble bunch!"

Harry hesitated. "I don't altogether blame them. I hate to think what the Sharkes will do if they catch us, and I'm not sure where to go, either. I can't go home. And how does one set about breaking away in broad daylight? If only I'd read a book or something about it."

The refusals had made Harry wonder whether they were, in fact, being ridiculously foolhardy. Laura was never wishy-washy, and was seldom plagued, as Harry was, by seeing all sides of a question.

"Where to go is no problem: you come home with me, of course. How to do it is simple. One, we get away from this mysterious trip before we drown. Two, we find help and rescue the others. Three, we spend the rest of the summer in glorious Chicago. I've had enough of uninhabited forests."

Laura had been talking without moving her lips, but now she noticed that Diana-Discipline was looking hard in her direction. She picked up the load of prime rib destined for the Sharke boat, and reflected that if there was one thing they had all learned at Camp Nish Na Bosh Na, it was how to become ventriloquists.

Coralene Sharke appeared in a sailing outfit of white with puce piping, and minced her way to the cabin cruiser. "Now," she decreed from the top of the gangplank, "all you little dears must run and get your sleeping bags. We are going to take a trip to some unknown lakes, to enjoy nature pure and undefiled, as the great poet says."

The children ran back, and returned with the outworn prison issue.

"By height, line hup," commanded D-Discipline.

Laura bent her knees a little. Gwen bent her knees a lot, and sagged in the middle as well. Harry stood on a friendly rock. Together they managed to be assigned to one canoe. Acorn, the smallest boy, was left over. Wearing a curious lump around his middle, he made his way to Harry and Laura's boat.

Egbert emerged from his cabin leading Danger. The dog lunged at the boats, her tongue out, sniffing hopefully. The children cringed, fearing the worst. Coralene took advantage of the scene to say, "See what Danger would do to any dear little boys or girls who tried to leave the group and go off by themselves? We would be quite unable to stop the animal from tearing those children limb from limb. That is, if the Minnesota rattlers hadn't bitten first." Harry gave a broad wink with his far eye at Acorn, who was looking alarmed. The boy brightened and attempted to wink back, which involved screwing up his face and shutting both eyes tight. Acorn thus avoided seeing the great dog make straight for their boat, tongue out and jaws dripping. With some difficulty, and more than a few curses, Egbert succeeded in tugging Danger away from the prow of Laura and Harry's canoe, and tied her below deck. Then he put down his large stack of luxurious lemon decorator tissues, a new brand he had found in the drugstore, and started swearing at the engine.

Meanwhile, Diana-Discipline leaped into her canoe, saying in bracing tones, "Follow me, children. The devil take the hindermost." She paddled energetically across the lake, followed by a straggle of leaky canoes.

20

Later in the day the deserted camp had several visitors. First, a telegraph boy from Minor Falls wobbled down the track. "Good grief," he said when he had called into every building. "Not a soul. All this way for nothing? Well, they can't say I didn't try." Another thought struck him. "Maybe they're all away on an overnight?"

He took three telegrams from his pouch and tacked them to the door of the biggest and best of the sorry group of cabins, which happened to be Coralene's. "They can't miss it there," he said. He gave a last look around, shrugged his shoulders, and pedaled back the way he had come.

The next visitor arrived in a huge green Chrysler Imperial. He pursed his lips and looked most put out. "Don't tell me the birds have flown?" he grumbled, pulling down a telegram addressed to Laura Lewis and opening it. "MONEY COMING WHY NEEDED TOUR TERRIFIC LOVE LYDIA."

The second one was for Harry Lewis. He opened that too, without a qualm. "DO WRITE HAVE HEARD NOTHING LOVE TO ADELAIDE AND YOU MOTHER AND DAD."

The third was addressed to Ames Oakes V. That one read: "DARLING ACORN WHEREVER ARE YOU STOP PLEASE CALL COLLECT TONIGHT STOP HOPE YOU ARE HAVING FUN AND MAKING FRIENDS STOP DO KEEP WARM AND DRY YOU KNOW WHAT YOUR COLDS ARE LIKE STOP WE ALL MISS YOU SWEETEST LAMBKIN HUGS AND KISSES MOLLY AND OAKEY."

James Dubious crumpled the telegrams, put them in his pocket, and bumped back along the track at eight miles to the gallon, pondering his next move.

The third visitor was an elderly woman with a battered tweed fishing hat crammed on unruly white hair, who walked along the lake path attacking weeds with her blackthorn walking stick as if they were personal enemies. She looked around the deserted camp with disapproval in her formidably intelligent gray eyes.

"Tut tut. To think how spick and span this place used to be. I wonder what Lydia can have been writing about? From the looks of things the camp was certainly not reopened, though I should dearly like to know who gave permission to use my name. Curious efforts to repair the dock, though, and some hoboes must have been using the cabins. What a pity the place ever closed. All those rumors spread by Nellie Highly, wanting to buy the place cheaply. Rabid wolves, indeed! I'd give her rabid wolves. If Minor

Falls hadn't diverted their sewage outlet at about the same time, she'd be sitting here now running some inefficient apology for a summer camp, or helping her nephew, James, to carve the place into fifty-foot lots. You could never trust the Highlys an inch, and their cousins, the Dubiouses, are even worse."

With that, she stumped off around the lake.

21

The canoes advanced across the water behind the cabin cruiser like a flotilla of ugly ducklings. The children were all paddling valiantly, afraid of what would happen to them if they lagged behind.

"If it weren't for the gunge in the water, this place would be pretty," said Laura. "Do you suppose all Minnesota lakes are full of green slime?"

"I saw 'Land of Sky Blue Waters' on a billboard in Basswood," offered Harry. "So I think there must be something wrong with this one."

"Can we escape yet?" asked Acorn.

"Shh," said Laura. "Don't mention the word. There's sure to be a chance before long."

"I wonder where they're taking us?" said Harry.

"Right through the Boundary Waters into Canada, to Lake Winnibigogmagog," answered Gwen unexpectedly. "I heard Egbert grumble about it to Coralene when he was getting the maps for his boat."

"Trust them," said Harry gloomily. "Minnesota has

ten thousand lakes—it says so on the license plates. It would take about three years to check them all. When you add the lakes in Canada, it's the perfect place to hide a whole kidnapped camp."

They were fast approaching the far shore, and there was no sign of a channel or any outlet from the lake.

"Row, you guys, row," roared Diana-Discipline, rounding up the stragglers. "Let's see some Olympic form."

Egbert popped up from his motor and dropped anchor.

"We are portaging from here to Gooseberry Lake. On the count of three, step out of your canoes and lift them onto your shoulders," instructed Diana-Discipline. "One, two, three!"

The children, presented with a choice between disobeying a Sharke, and the deep green, possibly bottomless lake, chose to obey. They stepped overboard and were distinctly relieved to feel mud squish between their toes. The boats were lifted and carried on aching shoulders through the woods to the next lake, where the campers threw themselves, exhausted, on a little beach.

"Now then, lazybones," exhorted Diana-D. "Up you get. The idle days are over. You have to earn your suppers. Back for another portage."

The children left their canoes and struggled back to where Coralene was standing on the bridge of the cruiser, spraying herself liberally with Eau de Nile.

"Such a stink," she said, waving the lacy ends of her headscarf. "It is all we can do to keep it at bay."

She tottered down the gangplank on her high heels and was off to the new lake without a backward glance.

Egbert appeared on deck. "I think I might just check a certain drop point," he said, with a yellowish grin. "On guard, Danger. Stay." He vanished through the trees, leaving behind a trail of used lemon tissues.

Diana-Discipline divided the children into two teams. One was given ropes to pull the Sharke Liner, as Laura had christened it. The other team pushed from behind. "This will count as today's exercise instead of pushups," Diana-D said with an air of benevolence.

"I feel like an Israelite slave, hauling stones for the pyramids," said Laura, panting.

"I feel like a prisoner of war, building the Burma road for the Japanese," puffed Harry.

"I'm hot and tired," said Gwen matter-of-factly. "My back aches and my hands are blistered. I can't go on much longer."

Acorn began to cry. For a while no one felt like cheering him up, but then Laura whispered, "Never mind, we're going to escape, remember?"

"Escape now?" asked Acorn loudly.

"Soon," promised Laura. "Shh."

At long last the heavy boat was pulled over the last ridge and pushed downhill into Gooseberry Lake.

"We hope you will be far quicker next time," said Coralene, yawning. "We've been waiting here for ages, and the mosquitoes are so tiresome."

Egbert came back with a satisfied smirk and a

brown attaché case, which he disappeared into the cruiser to open.

"All present and correct," he announced to his sisters as he reappeared. Turning to Acorn, he said, "Your Ma and Pa have done so well, I think we'll ask them for the same again. Thought you must be a poor relation. Didn't know quite what a big fish we had hooked. But who knows, they might not have wanted you back at all. I wouldn't altogether blame them."

Acorn looked bewildered. Laura's rage boiled up again.

"Steady the head," she said to herself. "No point in saying anything and ruining the chance of escape by getting chained up by Diana-D or whatever."

So instead, she imagined a large, rotten zucchini landing squash on Egbert's protruding nose and dripping down his ghastly face. Green and yellow. By the time it got to his smeared white shoes, Laura felt far better. Acorn, she noted, was sticking his tongue out, crossing his eyes, and making a truly horrible face behind Egbert's back.

22

Laura kept scanning the lake shore, hoping to catch sight of a possible rescuer or a place where they might dodge into hiding. It was discouraging work. Gooseberry Lake seemed to be empty of people and devoid of cabins or any other cover. The cruiser steered for the reeds marking the shallows at the far end, where a channel led to Little Fool Lake, farther north. The children paddled along behind it.

Suddenly there was a commotion among the boats. Diana-Discipline's whistle shrilled, and she was seen to be pointing her paddle toward a canoe that was slowly disappearing below the water. The campers all turned to converge on their sinking fellows.

"Now or never," said Laura. "Pull for the reeds, everyone."

"Kalamazoo," said Harry, paddling his hardest.

Gwen persuaded Acorn, who was tangling his paddle with the others in an effort to help, to crouch in the bottom, where he was less of a liability. She kneeled in the bow and pulled the reeds apart to make a passageway.

The boat glided in readily enough at first, where the reeds were far apart, but slowed down where they grew more densely. The children were barely hidden from the lake before it became impossible to nose the canoe any deeper into the reed bed.

"Good soldiers never panic." Harry fished his hat out from under his sweat shirt. "They weigh the odds, coolly." All the same, as he settled the hat on his head he could feel panic surging up from the pit of his stomach. The odds weren't anything to write home about.

"We must move farther in," urged Laura. "They'll miss us any moment now, and I don't want that awful Egbert to come and find us sitting in the rushes like paralyzed rabbits."

Gwen slipped over the side without a word. The lake was deeper than it seemed; it came up to her shoulders. Acorn gave a frightened gasp. "I can't swim. I don't even like putting my head under water." He opened his mouth wide, as if to howl in protest.

"Shh," whispered Laura. "Don't worry, we aren't going to make you get out."

Away from the influence of the Sharkes Gwen seemed a different person, much more lighthearted. "This is a job for human beanpoles, Acorn. You don't qualify," she said. "I'll find out where it starts getting shallow enough for us all to wade ashore." With a hasty wave, Gwen pushed her way through the reeds and away from the canoe.

The reeds closed behind her. They looked at each other. The afternoon became hot and oppressive. A pair of redwinged blackbirds buzzed and rasped from a perch nearby, offended by invaders in their territory.

"Look," said Harry in a low voice. "With those stripes on their shoulders they could be bird sergeants, giving orders and making lots of noise about it."

"They sound more like a pair of Diana-Disciplines to me," said Laura. "Just think of two of her."

"Yech," said Acorn, with feeling.

"Shh," said Harry and Laura, together.

Gwen seemed to have been gone for a dreadfully long time. The children listened tensely for sounds of her return, or for indications from the lake that their absence had been discovered.

"You don't think Coralene has caught her and is coming to get us next?" asked Acorn, his lower lip trembling.

"Of course not," answered Laura, beginning to wish Acorn was in some other boat. "We would have heard anything like that."

Acorn was reassured, and started to examine his sunburn. Laura began to worry that Gwen had stepped into a hole, and that the weeds were, even now, wrapping themselves around her body. Harry had a vision of Egbert gagging Gwen and creeping silently up on the canoe. The relief they all felt at the splashing sounds of her return was enough to overcome their alarm at the whistle blasts and distant shouts that announced, all too clearly, that they had been missed.

Gwen emerged from the reeds like a friendly beaver, shaking the wet from her hair and smiling from ear to ear. Laura suddenly realized that she had only once seen Gwen smile before — in the gravel pit where they had found the strawberries. Camp Nish Na Bosh Na did not promote cheerfulness.

"I found a hidden channel that I think will give us a way out," said Gwen, catching the prow of the boat and guiding it into the maze of cattails and bulrushes. The sounds of the search were growing louder and nearer. Laura, Harry, and Acorn tugged on the reeds to give them a little extra momentum. For a while they seemed to be making painfully slow progress, but at last they shot into a patch of clear water. Gwen pointed out a leaf moving gently with the current. "Look, it's floating away from Gooseberry Lake. This must be an outlet that Coral Reefs didn't know about."

"Perhaps it's only here when there's been a lot of rain and the lake is extra high," suggested Harry, glad the downpours and wet sleeping bags had not been entirely in vain.

The canoe lurched and threatened to tip over as Gwen climbed in again, water streaming off her Iowa State Boys' Reform School shirt and Sharke shorts.

"Paddle for dear life," commanded Laura.

Harry felt a moment's irritation that Laura seemed to see herself as captain of their craft. He wore the lieutenant's hat, and it was obvious to him that commanding the boat was a boy's job. That would have to be settled later. For the moment, the thought of facing the fury of Diana-Discipline, or, even worse, Coralene dripping sugary venom, was enough to make them all paddle as though they had been doing it all their lives. Somehow they found a rhythm that sent them turning and twisting along the little watercourse, their heads ducked well below the top of the reeds on either side. The canoe edged between two fallen tree trunks and their paddles struck a sandbar. Harry and Laura grinned at each other. Coralene and Egbert were certainly going to be stuck in the Sharke Liner, if ever they found the secret exit from the lake.

The little current became stronger, and the fugitives rested their paddles and let the canoe drift. They examined their blisters. Laura was pleased to find that hers were the largest. That helped the pain considerably. She watched a hummingbird hover near a scarlet swamp flower and then, with invisible wing-beats, dart away over a patch of wild rice.

The canoe stuck on a mudbank. Harry hopped over the side. The minnows tickled his toes as he pushed the boat into deeper water. He watched their transparent bodies flicking to and fro, while Gwen patiently undid the Olympic-style knots of Laura's hated placard. When at last it came free, Harry pushed it deep into a hole in the bank. "Rural-route delivery for Miss D-Discipline," he said.

They all giggled, and then took deep breaths of the marsh smell around them. It was sort of ripe and rotten, but in a pleasing way. And at last it dawned on them how still everything was. The sounds from the lake had quite died away.

"Couldn't we stop here?" pleaded Acorn.

Laura was glad he had asked. She was aching for a rest, but had not wanted to seem feeble to Harry and Gwen. Riding a bicycle in the Chicago suburbs did not prepare one adequately for paddling through the spillways of Minnesota lakes.

"Better not," said Harry. "We must go on until we have a proper hiding place."

They rounded the next bend and saw something surprising. A wooden trestle bridge crossed their stream. Harry smothered a pang of disappointment. He had thought they were in unexplored territory, never before seen by human eyes.

"Good," said Laura, keeping her eye on their main purpose. "Now we can go along the road until we reach help."

"Wait," said Harry. "What if the first people we meet are the Sharkes, waiting up there for us to show ourselves?"

"They're on the cabin cruiser," objected Laura. "They won't be here. I bet they think we got ahead of them."

"It's not safe," persisted Harry. "They might have split up to catch us again. We've got to wait till dark."

"Nonsense," said Laura, wishing her cousin would stick to being a quiet, bookish, unpractical type and quit making suggestions as if he were the officer in charge. "We can't waste any time. We must call the police right away, or heaven knows what will happen to the other kids. Come on, Gwen."

Gwen hesitated awkwardly. "I think Harry has a point," she said.

Acorn looked at his shoes, hoping he wouldn't be asked to take a side. The laces were undone as usual.

"All right," said Laura ungraciously. "Let's go on and enlarge our blisters."

She seized her paddle and dug it into the water with ostentatious energy. It really was too bad of the others to gang up on her like this. She had found at home that things went far better if she was in charge. That way there was no panic about being late, or leaving the swimming towels behind. Laura had become so used to organizing her mother that she found it difficult to believe that anyone else could have good ideas about how things should be done.

Beyond the bridge, the stream trickled into a shallow, round lake—a sort of glorified farm pond with a collar of sedges and reeds surrounding rafts of water lilies. The trees came right down to the water's edge.

"We have to avoid the trestle road and make our way through the woods. That road could be an enemy ambush," said Harry. Commanding officers must make prompt decisions, and it stood to reason that the oldest boy should be the commanding officer. He touched his lieutenant's hat, glad to feel it back in its rightful place.

"I can't walk an inch, especially through woods, when there's a perfectly good road up there," said Laura crossly. Who was Harry to be giving orders?

She was the one who had engineered this escape, at least she had given the signal.

They looked at Acorn. He was fast asleep in the bottom of the boat, the satin ribbon of his grubby blanket clutched in his hand.

"Let's all take a rest," suggested Gwen, the peacemaker, "and give the Sharkes time to move on. Then perhaps we can follow the road to the nearest town. It might be difficult finding our way through the woods."

They pushed and paddled the canoe back into the reeds that circled the round pond, until they were well hidden. The stillness returned. Two muskrats continued their interrupted task of building a larder in the bank. A coot scooted her chicks from their hiding place out onto the open water, and a duck appeared, with a train of ducklings behind her that looked like the bumps of a water serpent.

"What a super place to read. I wish I had a book," Harry said. He flung himself back to watch the small, woolly white clouds drift across the pale blue northern summer sky.

Through the tracery of wild rice, five feet above her head, Laura examined a light haze of gnats dancing over the boat. She was the only one awake to hear the snap of a turtle and the frantic squawking of the mother duck rushing her ducklings for cover. Finally, Laura could no longer stay on guard, and she too fell asleep.

23

The sleeping children stirred and woke at more or less the same time. Acorn scrunched up his Nice-and-Cosy, which Gwen had spread over him before she went to sleep to protect his already burned and peeling skin from the sun.

. "I'm hungry," he announced. "Look, there are plates for our dinner." He pointed to the water-lily pads.

Gwen reached out a long arm to pick one for him. She only managed to rock the boat, so Laura fished out her Swiss army knife and cut Acorn a plate. She turned it over to show him the purple underside. "Here you are, your majesty, a plate fit for a king."

Laura cut a plate for each of the others.

"What shall we put on them?" asked Acorn.

Harry shared out his last carrot flakes. "I think they'll expand in your stomach. Drink some water and you'll feel fuller in a while," he assured Acorn, although he wasn't by any means fully persuaded that a few dried carrot flakes could fill the gaping hole he felt inside.

"If only I had spent my money on condensed food at that place in Basswood, instead of saving it," sighed Laura. "Lydia—that's my mother—always says it's never our extravagances that come back to haunt us, but the times when we were too sensible to take a risk. She's a bit extravagant, actually, but perhaps she's right. Harry, did that plant book of yours tell what to eat while starving in the wilderness?"

"Diana-Discipline took it before I had time to read it properly. I can remember bits, but the trouble is that I can't recall the plant descriptions and pictures. I might give you all some deadly poison, like Diana-D and her mushrooms."

"I can recognize some plants," offered Gwen. "My grandmother used to name them for me, but I don't think she ate them a whole lot."

"Well," said Harry, "the book said that the young shoots of the cattail rushes afford some of the finest eating in the wild. Are these things sedges, bulrushes, cattails, or what?"

"That's easy," said Gwen. "Cattails. See that pale brown untidy part? That becomes the dark cattail later in the summer."

"Great," said Laura, fishing out her knife again.

Harry and Gwen tried to tug up a reed, but the plant stayed obstinately anchored in the mud and the canoe threatened to tip over. So Laura cut the stalk at water level and looked curiously at the rings of green getting paler and paler toward the center, a bit like a leek. Watched by six hopeful eyes, she peeled off two outside layers and nibbled cautiously on the third. It was tough and stringy. She spat it out and peeled off several more rings before she tried again. This time the stalk was tender and pale green and tasted faintly of onions. Finest eating among wild plants or not, it would do. She chopped several lengths for the others.

Harry, who had been debating whether their need of the spaghetti dinner would be greater now or later, found his appetite winning over his caution, in a way his aunt Lydia might have approved. He opened the tube and they all tried it, first on the cattail pieces and then on their fingers. Either way, they found that a dehydrated spaghetti dinner tastes pretty bad; but it did help the hunger pains, and, as Laura pointed out, kids who had eaten Sharke food could eat anything.

Acorn leaned over the edge and watched a waterbug zigzagging madly across the surface. He was quite unworried by their predicament, because he was confident that the older children knew what they were doing.

"I wonder why it doesn't swim straight?" he asked.

Gwen peered at his bug. "I think they do it so the fish won't be able to catch them."

"Evasive action," said Harry. "Commandos. Like us."

They all leaned over the water, watching the waterbugs. As their eyes got used to looking into the lake, they could see minnows frisking through the reed stems, and a brown pike lurking under the weeds.

"Oh, can't we catch it?" cried Laura. She reached down, but the pike whisked away. "Shouldn't we be moving on?"

Harry took a careful survey of the lake, to make sure no Sharkes were watching them. "I wonder what that is?" He pointed out an untidy heap of twigs and branches across the largest patch of clear water.

"It's probably an old beaver lodge," said Gwen, who knew more than anyone had guessed. "They have them in Wisconsin, too. That one must be abandoned; look at the way the willow twigs have rooted and are growing green on top."

"Oh, I've always wanted to see a beaver," said Acorn, his eyes shining. "Can we paddle over to it?"

"No," said Harry and Laura together, although they too would have liked to inspect the beaver lodge.

"We must keep hidden," Harry explained. "The Sharkes may have found some way of getting back to their bus. If we wait until Egbert has to use his headlights, we'll be able to see him coming and hide before he can see us."

And so it was getting dark before the escape party dared to push the canoe from the hiding place to the bank, and scrambled up to the trestle bridge.

24

The road was not at all what they had expected.

"It's only another track, like the one to Nish Na Bosh Na," groaned Laura, feeling badly let down. "Do you think there are any regular roads in northern Minnesota?"

"It must be an old logging road," said Gwen. "There was one near where my grandmother lived. She told me that timber was once cut all through the North Woods, before the lumber companies moved on to California and Oregon."

"Perhaps this leads to a ghost town," suggested Laura, and was immediately sorry, as Acorn paled and clutched his blanket for comfort.

"Not *those* ghosts, Silly Billy," she said hastily. "That's just a name for old, abandoned settlements. If this is a logging road," she told Harry and Gwen, "it's bound to join a proper road, or town, or railway track, or something. So let's go."

"Right," said Harry, looking worried. "The question is, which way? A logging road may join a proper road at one end, but I guess the other end just leads deeper into the woods. We'd better go toward the sunset."

Laura looked to where there was a little light left in the sky. It didn't look at all promising. "Oh dear," she said. She looked back to where the trestle bridge crossed the stream to the round pond. It seemed marginally less forbidding than the way forward. "No, I'm sure the nearest town must be back there," she said, pointing in the direction opposite Harry's.

The cousins glared at each other, neither willing to give in. Gwen broke the stalemate.

"Since we haven't a clue as to the right way, why don't we spin Harry's cap and go the way it points?"

Harry took off his cap and spun it. The peak pointed west, Harry's way. Laura bit her lip.

"Now, Laura, girl," she said to herself. "It's your own father's hat. You know how you hate for people to agree to something and then squabble if the results don't go their way."

They set off toward the last glimmers of the setting sun, walking with their eyes to the ground, to avoid obstacles and spot berries (Gwen had spied some on the bank of the round pond), and keeping their ears alert for the sound of a VW bus. It was tiring, trudging over rough clumps of grass and through the tall weeds that had invaded the old road, but they soon realized it was better than struggling through the woods without a path.

Harry tried to determine where they were. If only

he concentrated hard enough, he might be able to recall the shapes of lakes and the positions of towns from the map he had seen in Basswood. He wished he could share his worries, but Laura was obviously feeling sore about the direction they had taken. He wondered how a soldier landed behind enemy lines would behave. You probably had to keep your concerns to yourself: telling them would only enlarge the common pool of fears. What a pity, though, that Laura didn't understand about boys having to be the leaders.

Laura walked along in dread that they had taken the wrong way and were heading deeper into the wilderness. Acorn certainly would not be able to walk far. Perhaps they should split up and go by twos in different directions — or would that be even more dangerous, out in the wilds like this? She wanted to discuss the problem, but no longer seemed to be on good terms with Harry. And there was no point in upsetting Acorn. He cried all too easily as it was.

"I can't go any farther," said Acorn, and sat down.

Gwen kneeled down and tied up his shoelaces. "It doesn't matter about the laces," he said. "Somebody at home was always doing them up for me, but I never trip over them. It's just that I'm tired of walking."

"Come on," said Gwen. "I'll give you a piggyback to the next bend."

At the next bend, Acorn agreed to walk to the bend after that, but the older three realized that they couldn't go much farther. The light was getting very weak, and it seemed wise to stop before it went altogether. They were going to have to face a night in the woods. Acorn began to cry from tiredness, hopelessness, hunger, the burning of his sunburn, and the itching of his mosquito bites. He sat down on the track and wept for his mother as if his heart would break. The others felt their eyes prickling as they thought of their own mothers.

"We'll be eaten by wolves, like little Willie," sobbed Acorn.

"Oh do shut up, Acorn. You're just making things worse," snapped Laura, and immediately felt awful. She had always thought of herself as a kind, tolerant person, and here she was shouting at a first-grader.

Harry, who had gone ahead to explore the logging road, hurried back. "I think I've found somewhere we can spend the night," he announced.

Acorn dried his eyes and wiped his nose on his sleeve.

"Just around this bend, there's a group of sheds," Harry continued. "I think they must belong to an old sawmill. Anyway they'll be shelter for tonight. No ghosts anywhere, Acorn."

The children made their way to where a group of buildings loomed black against the lighter gray of the last twilight. Harry led them to one that was smaller and better built than the others. "I think it must have been the office," he said.

"Whatever it was, it's twice as good as anything we slept in at Nish Na Bosh Na," said Laura. "I'm beginning to think there's nothing but ruins in the North Woods."

"I wish we had a fire and something to eat," said Acorn, beginning to sniffle again.

Harry pulled out his trump card, the beef cube. With the smallest, sharpest blade of her knife, Laura carefully divided it into four equal parts. There wasn't much to munch.

Suddenly a startling sound split the stillness. Acorn clutched Harry.

"It's Egbert, telling Diana-D he can't find us and has gone mad with the effort," said Harry, trying to make them laugh.

Acorn's eyes were the size of saucers as the noise came again. "Don't worry," said Gwen. "It's only the cry of a loon."

"A loon?" asked Laura.

"It's a bird you find on the northern lakes," explained Gwen. "I always used to listen for it with my grandmother. I wondered why it never visited the lake at Nish Na Bosh Na. Didn't care for the water, I guess."

They were sitting with their backs to the wall of the old mill office, not wanting to go inside and risk having Egbert creep up and trap them there.

"I think we should take watches," said Harry in his best lieutenant's voice, tilting his cap in an authoritative fashion.

This irritated Laura, who said, "How silly. In the middle of an uninhabited forest like this?"

But Gwen agreed with Harry, and Acorn seemed to think his suggestions were law, so Laura shrugged and gave in. Privately, she thought it wasn't a bad idea. Among these endless trees, some of Harry's notions seemed to work better than hers. If only they were back among the familiar streets of Chicago. Then she could show them!

"Be honest, Laura," she told herself sternly. "Gwen knows a lot more useful things about this place than you do, and Harry was quite right about remaining hidden. Perhaps you shouldn't be deciding things for everyone." "Mmm," said herself, "but you've always been so good at it, Laura."

Trying to regain the feeling of being in control of things, she said aloud, "Well, I think you guys had better try to sleep. I'll take the first watch."

She jumped up and began to walk back and forth in a businesslike way. The others went inside, and Laura began to feel lonely. She kept a wary eye out for wolves, rabid skunks, poisonous snakes, and Indian war parties. She was fairly certain they had all been invented by Coralene to discourage escape attempts, but her confidence began to ebb away as she listened to the odd creaks and rustles and snaps in the darkness. The forest was far from empty. Five hundred toads or frogs creaked and trilled. There was a loud, but soft, "Ohoo, O-hoo," like the coo of a giant dove. Laura sat down, hoping the wildlife was of a size and temper to mind its own business and ignore visiting children. All in all, it was a huge relief when her cousin came over and sat beside her.

"Oh, Harry, I'm so hungry, aren't you?" she said. "And these awful mosquitoes! I once heard someone say they should be the Minnesota state bird.

The mosquitoes in Illinois aren't half as bloodthirsty."

They sat for a while in a companionable silence, watching the fireflies dance in and out of the trees.

"Why weren't there any lightning bugs at Nish Na Bosh Na?" Laura wondered aloud. "Noxious gases, I guess," she said, answering her own question. "You know, Harry, I was feeling a little scared of the woods, so I'm really glad you're here. It isn't scary at all with someone sitting beside you. Now the rustles seem friendly, somehow; and look at the moon. I don't ever remember seeing it look so beautiful."

Gwen came to join them, and after her trailed Acorn, complaining that he couldn't sleep.

"Look at the moon, Acorn," said the patient Gwen. "I've heard that Indians call it the Rose Moon."

"Oh," wailed Acorn. "The Indians—I'd forgotten. They'll scalp us."

"No, they won't," said Laura. "That was just Coralene's tale to frighten us."

"You know, I was once given an Indian name," said Gwen.

"What was it?" asked Laura.

"High Silver Pine. I've always been a beanpole," Gwen said, laughing a little ruefully.

"Indian names reflect their owners, don't they? I wonder what mine would be if I were an Indian?" Laura said. She mused over some beautiful, romantic names she would have liked.

"Nish Na Bosh Na. Dancing water," suggested Harry.

"Thank you," said Laura stiffly, a little hurt. "But isn't there some other lake? I'm not that bad, you know."

Harry laughed, and Laura realized she was being teased.

"Morning Star," said Gwen suddenly. "That's you."

Morning Star? It wasn't quite what Laura had been thinking of, but as she repeated it to herself she liked it more and more. Morning Star. Her mother would like to call her that sometimes. Laura was always the first one up in their household.

Acorn was bouncing up and down in his eagerness to get a word in. "And me? What would I be called?"

"Jumping Mouse," said Laura.

"Jumping Green Mouse," added Gwen, seeing Acorn's comforter wound around his arm.

"And me?" asked Harry. "Mighty Tomahawk?"

"More like Gray Otter," said Gwen.

"Why Gray Otter?" asked Harry.

"I don't know," said Gwen. "It just sounds right."

Harry was silent. He didn't quite understand why Gwen thought the name fitted him, but he felt it was important and he would puzzle it out later.

"Let's be Indians," said Acorn.

"We can't be. We aren't," said Laura.

Acorn sniffled, but to their relief he didn't start crying.

"I wish we knew some Indian secrets like lighting a fire," said Harry, slapping at the mosquitoes. "I hate these things."

Gwen handed him a frond of bracken. "I suddenly

realized I was sitting on this stuff people wave around to keep off the flies. It might work for mosquitoes, too," she said. She handed more bracken to the other two, and they waved the leaves violently at first, but then with less enthusiasm as the mosquitoes pierced their leafy defenses.

"Listen," said Harry. They listened. The wind sounded like a vast gentle sea above them, and the loons renewed their calls across the water as clearly as if they were a pebble-throw away.

"Why do loons make such a funny noise?" asked Acorn.

Harry remembered a book of Indian legends he had once read, and so he told them how two lovers who used to call across the lake to each other were changed into loons when they died.

"How beautiful," said Morning Star, when he had finished.

"How sad," said High Silver Pine.

Jumping Green Mouse said nothing at all. He was fast asleep.

"Look," said Harry. "Let's forget this watch business. The Sharkes are probably asleep too."

They roused Acorn and walked back to the shelter of the lumber office, where they all settled down, huddled together for warmth and comfort.

25

The children awoke next day feeling free as field mice. They lay listening to the sounds of the forest—the bird songs and the whispering of the pine boughs—secure in the knowledge that Diana-Discipline's loathsome whistle would not shatter the peace.

"We have escaped the Jaws of the Sharkes," announced Harry, and Acorn almost split his sides laughing.

"Getting up gets easier and easier," gurgled the heir to the Oakes millions. "First no washing and dressing, and now no beds and breakfast. It seems funny to go straight into the day like this."

Harry, trying to avoid a leader-of-the-troops voice, coughed and said, "Just in case the Terrible Three come tracking us, I think we should clear up all traces of our being here."

To Harry's relief, Laura made no objection. They got to their feet and looked around to see what should be hidden. The place where they had sat looking at the moon and listening to the loons was the obvious giveaway. Laura began to scatter the wilted bracken fronds, while Gwen went off to find something that would convincingly cover the flattened vegetation. She found a branch that might do the job, and was bending down to fluff up the scuffed grass around it when large drops of blood started plopping on the gray surface of the rock Harry had been leaning against the previous night. "Oh dear, not again," Gwen said. She put her head back and tried to pinch the bridge of her nose. The others gathered around, concerned.

"Don't worry," said Gwen indistinctly. "I often get nosebleeds. At home they used to put a cold key down my back, and say it was because I was growing so fast."

The others offered helpful, and not-so-helpful, ideas. Laura made a plug of moss, to try and staunch the flow. Harry suggested that she lie down, and had the vague feeling that he should be bringing his hat full of water. Had he read that somewhere?

"If only we'd swiped some of Egbert's Kleenex," sighed Laura.

At long last, Gwen's nose decided to stop. By this time there was a good deal of blood around, and Acorn was looking a little green.

"I wish," said Harry, "that I had a magic lamp you could rub and make a hot shower appear."

A more practical notion struck Laura instantly. "Why don't we go and swim in that lake?" She pointed to the left of the buildings, where they could see a patch of distant water dancing in the sun. "It doesn't look far. We're all pretty grubby, and it would be nice to clean up. If Coralene's cabin cruiser appears, we can always scoot back into the woods."

It was a terrific idea. The four of them immediately headed for Laura's lake. Acorn skipped and jumped from patch to patch of sunlight. "The bears catch you if you step in the shadow," he told them.

Laura couldn't help a hasty glance into the shade. No bears, thank goodness. And no Sharkes, either; double thank goodness. Through the birches at the forest edge, they could see the lake clearly now, glinting blue and inviting, and they broke into a run.

As they came out of the woods, a great gray-blue bird, which had been standing hunched over the water some distance from the shore, took off with slow, clumsy wingbeats. They watched it fly away along the margin of the lake.

"It looks too heavy to fly, like a boat in the air. What is it? Is that an eagle?" asked Acorn.

"It's a great blue heron. I expect he was fishing in the shallows for his breakfast," answered Gwen.

"Good," said Laura. "That means we don't have to worry about the water being too deep for Acorn."

They raced down the bank and splashed into the lake. It was cold at first, but exciting cold, not icy cold. They waded out, through a sort of underwater mirror of the forest behind them, to the clear water of the sandbank where the heron had been fishing.

Laura looked at her feet. The ripples broke the sunlight into octagonal patterns of light on the lake

bottom, and then the pattern broke into bright frag-
ments as the children splashed each other and washed
away every last trace of the nosebleed, and of the
murky waters of Nish Na Bosh Na. Acorn, who seemed
to be having no trouble getting his head under the
water, dived for Harry's toes. Laura picked up some
shells and wondered what kind of lake snails had
inhabited the delicate, mother-of-pearl spirals. She
watched long-legged Gwen imitating the heron to
amuse Acorn, and squinted at a handsome pair of
birds in the distance. They seemed to be swans.

"If only it were all like this, I might even get to
like Minnesota almost as much as Chicago," Laura
was thinking, splashing blissfully, when a plane
began to circle the lake.

The swimmers dived for the woods.

"I didn't dream the Sharkes would get a plane to
search for us," confessed Harry as they watched it
search the lake.

"I expect it's my father looking for me," said Acorn.
"I think we should go out and wave."

The others were touched by the little boy's faith in
his father to work miracles.

"But your father doesn't know where you are,"
Laura pointed out.

"We daren't risk it, Acorn," said Harry. "It's sure
to be Egbert up there."

Rather subdued, they returned to the logging road,
a little way from the old lumberworks. Laura was the
first to emerge from the trees. She looked casually
right and left, not so much because she expected to

see something as because looking both ways before crossing a road was hammered into city children at a tender age. She stiffened. The others, catching up with her and following her gaze, froze. In front of them, in the middle of the green road, lay a crumpled lemon tissue.

"That wasn't here before," said Laura uncertainly.

They looked toward the deserted sawmill. There was no sign of the VW bus. "How lucky. Egbert must have driven by while we were swimming," said Laura, rather proud that she had managed to get everyone safely out of harm's way.

"What's that?" asked Gwen, pointing at a gray-ish green heap lying in the open outside the office building.

"However did my Nice-and-Cosy get out there?" asked Acorn in surprise. "I hid it like you told me to."

He moved forward to rescue it, but Laura caught his arm. "Wait, Acorn. It may be a trap. What if Danger nosed out your blanket and Egbert is hidden in the shed at this very minute, waiting to grab you when you pick it up?"

"What should we do, then?" asked Acorn, his eyes filling with tears.

"Leave it there and get away from here as fast as we can," answered Laura promptly, taking command.

Harry felt cross that she hadn't given him a chance. He had intended to propose that. "All right, Miss Bossy," he said angrily.

Laura flushed. It hit a very sore spot with her. She decided she was tired of Harry's assumption that boys were the rightful leaders. Girls were usually twice as competent, in her experience. "I suppose you think that nobody has the right to give orders but General Harry Lewis?" she said.

"Look," said Gwen, "don't you think we should get out of here now and argue later? After all, Egbert Sharke is probably waiting for us right over there, and Danger may catch our scent any minute."

Laura and Harry looked a little sheepish. "Sorry," they both muttered.

"As soon as we get help, we'll come back for your blanket, I promise," added Gwen to Acorn.

"Okay," replied Acorn, swallowing a lump in his throat.

"If Egbert knows where we spent the night," Gwen continued, "he may have sent for the Ugly Sisters. So we must keep away from the road."

They faded back into the woods like Indians (they hoped), and set off in the opposite direction.

26

"Damn and blast," said Egbert, emerging from his hiding place two hours and a box of Kleenex later. "I could have sworn those kids would come back for the blanket." He whistled. "Here, Danger. You don't get that bone after all, you dopey pooch."

Danger wagged her tail enthusiastically on hearing the familiar name. Her owner kicked Acorn's comforter aside contemptuously. As he did so, he caught sight of something dark red on the ground.

"What the blazes . . . ? Bloody murder! Let me out of this." He ran for the bus, which was parked discreetly in one of the larger sheds.

At midday, a jeep clattered up to the old lumber mill. Two policemen from the station at Basswood got out.

"Hey kids!" the tall one shouted, putting his hands to his mouth. "Hullo there! Anyone at home?"

"That Oakes woman is crazy," said his partner.

"You don't just kidnap a whole camp of children. Anyway, there are no signs of kids spending the night here: no campfire, no candy wrappers, no scorched marshmallows, no peanuts, no nothing. The only recent marks that I can see are those tire tracks. Probably made by a forestry worker doing the rounds."

The first policeman poked around a bit and turned over a not-quite-natural-looking pile of stones and twigs. Then he gave a low whistle. "Say, come and look at this."

They looked for a long moment at the blood.

"Good grief." The doubting officer had turned pale. "Those poor kids. C'mon, back to the station. We've got to get more than the county force onto this. We need the state troopers and maybe the FBI."

A minute later they roared off down the track.

The spotter plane, which had been patrolling the area all morning, now circled the disused lumber plant.

"Worth a look?" asked the pilot.

"Certainly," said his passenger.

The plane landed on the lake and taxied to shore. Two men got out and made for the old sheds.

"Funny thing Acorn doesn't wave to us," the passenger said. "He surely hears the plane. They can't be far away."

"Perhaps they think we're connected with the kidnappers," said the pilot, privately thinking of several far worse alternatives. "Hey, what's this?"

He held up a tattered green blanket with a satin ribbon border, which had been kicked underneath a log. Mr. Ames Oakes the Fourth, billionaire and friend of presidents, turned very white and sat down suddenly. The pilot decided this was not the right moment to mention the bloodstains.

"We must comb these entire woods, leaf by leaf, tree by tree. If necessary, employ every able-bodied person in northern Minnesota; I can afford it," said Acorn's father. "I'll phone the Pentagon and see if we can't get the army up here. Get hold of the governor for me, first thing."

The plane's takeoff was noted by the driver of a big green Chrysler. Mr. James Dubious gritted his teeth and looked for a turning place on the old logging road. "Worse than I feared," he muttered, accidentally hitting the horn as he slapped the flat of his palm on the steering wheel. "Some of the really big boys must be interested. That explains all the fresh tracks on this road. I'd better triple my offer to the stubborn old girl. The whole deal will slip through my fingers if I can't get her land. I wonder if she'd take the Nish Na Bosh Na place in a straight swap?"

"Wow," said the Basswood *Northern Light* reporter, who had got wind of something really big at the police station. She took out her note pad. "Now let's get this straight: Pools of blood? Billionaire's son? Famous singer's only child? Educational camp scandal? The entire army on alert? Secret Service involvement? Hundreds of kids abducted to Canada? Wowie, is this my chance! I can just see the headline: BABES IN THE WOODS."

27

After its bright start, the morning had become gray and misty, but toward noon the sun gradually burnt the clouds away and lifted the children's spirits. Lunch would have lifted them even higher. Gwen spotted a bush of chokecherries, but they turned out so puckery that the children felt as if their mouths were lined with bitter fur. A little farther on, she borrowed Laura's knife to cut some wild asparagus. It was stringy and hard to chew; Acorn spat his out. "We have it all the time at home. I hate it there, too," he complained.

Chewing spearmint leaves helped ease the hunger pains somewhat, but Laura would have given a forest of spearmint for one order of French fries.

"I once read that when the voyageur fur traders were traveling the Boundary Waters, they used to take ten minutes' 'pipe time' every hour, just to sit and smoke. Do you think that would be a good idea— the break, I mean?" asked Harry cautiously, not wishing to antagonize Laura.

"Sure," said Laura, who had decided not to squabble with her cousin, so long as he was reasonable. "Let's take two breaks; five minutes each half-hour. Acorn will need the rest."

In fact, Acorn was keeping up remarkably well; but as the day wore on, they were all increasingly glad to take the break, particularly Laura, who had a blister on her heel that was causing her considerable pain.

"Ouch! How awful. You poor thing!" exclaimed Gwen, catching sight of it. She made Laura a pad of soft yarrow leaves, which seemed to help, though it was her sympathy as much as the yarrow, which kept slipping, that made Laura feel better.

They dared not stop for longer than the agreed five minutes, for fear that Egbert and Danger might pick up their trail. Anyway, Laura, who was trying to keep track of the time, was afraid that if she stopped for a real rest she might never be able to get started again.

"The one good thing about mosquitoes," said Harry, "is that they make sitting down so miserable you're almost glad to get going again."

"Bugs on a log," announced Acorn at their next rest time. "I'm starving." He was sitting on one end of a fallen tree trunk.

The others looked at him, startled. It was true they were pretty hungry, but still—bugs?

"You know," he explained, "peanut butter filling up a stick of celery, and raisins on top. Cook makes it for me whenever I want."

"Oh, *those* bugs on a log," said Laura. "Yes, they're pretty good. You mean your mother makes them for you? You're supposed to do them for yourself."

"Look," Gwen said, and pointed to a sort of leaf propeller on a thin stem. "I think that's an Indian cucumber. It won't be as good as your bugs, Acorn, but it's time for a snack."

"Snackeroo," echoed Acorn, while Laura dug where Gwen suggested, and blessed her Swiss army knife yet again. She wondered what would happen if Acorn started demanding Indian cucumber snacks once he got back home. But having dug up the root, wiped it clean on her shirt, divided it into four, and tasted it, she decided Mrs. Oakes was unlikely to be asked.

"Why are the trees here dead at the bottom and alive at the top?" demanded Acorn, who seemed able to talk nonstop now that he was at a safe distance from Diana-Discipline.

"Struggle for light," said Harry, who dimly remembered a science lesson about the Amazon jungle. Acorn seemed satisfied.

"What did the ticks at Nish Na Bosh Na live on before we got there?" he wanted to know next.

Laura sighed, and no one had the energy to answer. They trudged on, puzzling about what the ticks could possibly have lived on, since they were so partial to campers' blood.

Harry found a good place for their next break: a clump of silver birch that was splayed out, so they could each lean against a trunk, with their feet touching in the middle and their heads far apart, gazing at the birch leaves quivering against the blue sky.

"I don't want to go any farther," announced Acorn.

"You have to," said Laura flatly, too tired to jolly him along.

Acorn looked as if he were about to start a sit-down mutiny. Harry tried to distract him. "Look, Jumping Green Mouse, you can peel off big pieces of this birch bark quite easily. The Indians used to use it for canoes and wigwam covers and paper and firelighting and lots of things. I once read an Indian story that told how the wings of the chickadee made those black marks on the trunk."

Acorn fingered the dark patches on his tree trunk. They did look like sooty wingprints.

"C'mon," said Laura. "Time to get going."

Acorn stuffed his pockets with curls of birch bark, just in case he needed to send messages or cover a wigwam, and followed the others. "Harry, why would a mouse be green?" he asked.

For the next break, they all sat on a tree stump that must have been two feet across. Harry tried to count the rings, but the wood was too darkened with damp and decay for him to see them properly. "Anyway, it must be at least two hundred years old," he said. "I wonder why this tree was so much bigger than all the others?"

"There were great stumps like this in Wisconsin," said Gwen. "I think the loggers cut down all the big trees years and years ago."

"I wish we could meet a woodcutter to help us,

like Little Red Riding Hood," said Acorn. This put his mind on stories, and he pleaded for somebody to tell him one.

Harry, who had been thinking about escapes, asked, "Would you like to hear about the wooden horse?"

"Yes," said Acorn. Then remembering his mother's rules he added, "Please."

So Harry told about the prisoners of war in Germany, who dug a getaway tunnel underneath a wooden horse they had put in the open, near the camp fence, and pretended to use for gymnastics. The story lasted through three breaks. Laura had a hazy memory of her father coaxing her to eat her eggs by telling a story of two mice called Eek and Squeak. The point, so far as she remembered, was to reward a few mouthfuls of horrible fried egg with some more of the tale. So, despite Acorn's pleas, she insisted they all walk their full half-hour to earn another installment of Harry's story about escaping prisoners.

"Just like us," said Acorn proudly.

When the story was over, Laura remarked, "When you said the wooden horse, I thought you were going to tell us about ancient Greece and Troy."

That reminded Harry of another book locked in Diana-Discipline's cupboard: *Heroes of the Spartan Wars*. He racked his brain for anything he knew about the Spartans and their austerity and tests of endurance.

"Only one meal a day," marveled Acorn, forgetting his hunger and remembering how his mother would

146

coax him to eat breakfast, lunch, and supper, with nourishing snacks in between.

"They don't sound very cheerful, but they certainly were tough," commented Laura. "Imagine a whole army running in full armor for four days, all the way to Athens."

The story about the Spartans almost made walking endlessly through the North Woods without food, except for the occasional nibble pointed out by Gwen, seem a trifling inconvenience. Laura gritted her teeth at the pain in her blistered heel, imagined a Spartan mother was watching her, and resolved not to complain. Acorn practiced being a Spartan boy from time to time, though not quite as frequently as the other three would have liked.

The afternoon got hotter, and Harry began to have doubts. If this was a taste of jungle warfare, did he really want to go into the army?

It was a more tiring business than any of them had imagined: pushing through the woods, following little twisting animal paths that petered out, being whipped in the face by bushes, and having balsam saplings catch in their hair. The oldest parts of the forest with the tallest trees proved easier going for them. The problem came in the more recent areas, where the undergrowth was thickest. They learned to skirt open patches, where the increased light encouraged thickets of young trees and briars.

Gwen came off best; she kept a watchful eye out for anything edible, and thus saw a good deal more of forest life than anyone else. When there was no story, and the others were concentrating on their aches and pains, on listening for the Sharkes, and on getting out of the woods, Gwen was the one who stopped to point out the rare blooms of the moccasin flower.

Acorn stroked the red-and-white velvet petals. "I wish these were magic moccasins. I'd put them on and lead us all out of the forest," he said.

Gwen also explained to Harry that he was looking at a moose print, when he thought it was a cow's hoof that promised a nearby farm.

"I would have known that, if only Diana-D hadn't swiped my animal-track book," Harry complained.

Gwen also spent a good deal of time helping Acorn, whom the others found rather a pain. She made him laugh by pointing out the nannyberry and bleating like a goat. When Acorn announced that he was sure there really were wolves behind the trees, she made him look for the neatly gnawed logs that were beavers' work, and suggested he look for porcupines instead of nonexistent wolves. "They're very shy, Acorn," she said. "It would be terrific to find one."

At one stop, kneeling on a rotting tree trunk to watch a pair of chipmunks, she said dreamily, "It's better to travel hopefully than to arrive. Grandmother used to say that," she explained to the others, who looked baffled.

"What nonsense," said Laura, thinking that with Harry daydreaming about jungle warfare, Gwen prepared to travel endlessly, and Acorn being somewhat unpredictable, it was just as well that one member of the group remembered what they were supposed to be doing. "It's the traveling that's our problem," she said. "Once we arrive at a telephone and tell people where we are, our troubles will be over."

"I know," said Gwen. "It's just that I was wondering what was going to happen after that. Do you think the Sharkes will be put in prison? Will we have to give evidence against them in court?"

"I wouldn't be surprised," said Laura. "They deserve it."

"I don't know about jail," said Harry, "but I would certainly put them on a remote island in the South Pacific for ten years, without a single thing to read, and only each other for company. I wish I could send a message to my parents to look out for a handy atoll."

"With a ten-year supply of rotten spinach to eat," said Laura.

"And lessons in cursive writing every day," added Acorn.

Harry had some idea that the Welsh and the Japanese ate moss, so they chose a granite boulder for their next stop, and Harry scraped away at its side. One chew was enough to make them decide that moss was out of the question for Americans, even such hungry ones.

"Perhaps it was seaweed they ate," amended Harry. "But look at how the moss is growing on one side of this rock. Doesn't it grow on the sheltered side? That's the south. We could use it as a compass."

Laura was doubtful, remembering Harry's confusion about seaweed and moss. She got up and looked at a few more boulders, and then announced, "It won't work. These rocks have moss on the other side."

Harry looked crestfallen, but Acorn jumped up from his seat in high excitement upon seeing a shiny vein Harry's scraping had uncovered. "A gold mine!" he shouted.

"I don't think it's real gold. There's something called fool's gold," Harry told him.

Harry did seem to know a lot. Laura decided she had better visit the Chicago Public Library more often. Her blistered heel was by now causing her so much pain that she could only hobble along by gritting her teeth, practicing Spartan endurance, and continually saying to herself, "Laura, my girl, just twenty more steps. Try to get to that bush over there. Just keep going while I count to fifty." At last, she had to stop the group while she attended to the heel, which was rubbed raw by this time. She felt a good deal discouraged at having to give in and slow everyone down.

"Oh dear, I used to be able to do things so well in Chicago, but here I seem so feeble. I don't know any of the useful things Gwen does, like how to find Indian cucumbers and to wave bracken to keep away the flies and mosquitoes. I can't tell stories like Harry. Even Acorn keeps up better than I do." She tried to laugh but was nearer tears.

Gwen looked up quickly. "I may know more about the North Woods, but I didn't have the guts to get away from the Sharkes," she said. "I have this stupid way of doing exactly what I'm told, and I was silly enough to believe their tales about wolves and angry Indians and so on. If any of us should have known better, I should have. If you want to know the truth, I'd much prefer being lost in the woods to being at Nish Na Bosh Na. I can't imagine how I stuck it out those two weeks until you came."

"You know, I would have spent the whole summer at that awful place, wishing I could go to a library and look up what to do, under Camps: Escape from Impossible Ones. I spend so much time thinking about all the possibilities that I never get around to doing anything, except in my own head," confessed Harry. "You saw that we could hide in the reeds, Laura, and without your keeping track of the time, I think we'd just stop going, and then we'd really be lost, like little Willy."

"I can't do anything either, Laura," said Acorn, giving up a vain attempt to tie his shoelaces, his lip trembling slightly.

"Of course you can, Acorn," said Laura warmly, her irritation with him forgotten. "You're our lucky bean, our mascot, and, for a little kid, you're really brave."

A pleased smile lit up Acorn's grubby face. It was true, Laura realized. They needed Acorn. The older ones would have done far more grumbling and worrying out loud if it hadn't been for Acorn's confidence that the other three knew what they were doing and would eventually get him out of the woods.

"So lead on, Macduff," said Harry, grinning affectionately at his cousin, with what Gwen had called his Gray Otter expression. "In fact, none of us could have got along on this escape without the others. Just thank your lucky stars that we aren't at the bottom of a lake in one of those leaky canoes."

At the next break, Acorn voiced the question the others had all been avoiding. "Harry, how long before we get out of these woods?"

"Not long now, Green Mouse," said Harry. "I think we might see something from the top of that rock." He pointed ahead to a great granite boulder, dumped by the ice long ago. Laura, who knew they were lost, sighed, but Acorn, who had been flagging, found the energy to run ahead of the others. Balancing on top of the rock, he called back in clear and happy tones, "I'm the king of the castle. You're right, I can see it. It's the road at last."

"The power of suggestion," said Laura in her most grown-up manner.

Harry tried to remember if you had to be in a desert to see a mirage. Gwen was more inclined to believe Acorn. She thought she had heard a car horn a little while back, but had not been certain enough to risk raising the others' hopes. Nevertheless, she picked three early raspberries and stored them, to console Acorn in case he'd been mistaken and they still had many miles to walk.

28

The three older children found precarious footholds on Acorn's rock and looked down at the black ribbon of what was, sure enough, a proper Minnesotan paved road.

"Race you there!" shouted Laura, blister forgotten, giddy with relief. She had been wondering for some time now if they were really going to get out safely.

Laura and Harry raced down to the road, each trying to be first. Gwen and Acorn ran behind, Gwen going slowly, to make sure that Acorn wasn't the last to arrive at his lovely road. They collapsed on the grassy verge, getting their breath back and waiting for a car to pass and pick them up.

"I think the first thing to do is phone the police, so they can go and rescue the others and arrest Coralene and Company," said Laura, automatically organizing things. "We'll ask the driver to drop us off at the first phone."

Harry was finding it easier not to resent a girl taking charge. Laura was undoubtedly good at it, just as he had turned out to be good at telling stories. A car passed with a single person in it. They waved eagerly, but it didn't slow down. The reporter from the *Northern Light* didn't even see them. She was mentally composing her copy, and planning an interview with the famous Ames Oakes the Fourth, as she raced to meet the deadline in Basswood.

"Quick, everyone, turn around and pretend to be gathering berries!" shouted Harry.

"Why?" Acorn protested, but Gwen's long arm swung him around.

Mr. James Dubious sailed past without a glance.

"My goodness," said Laura. "How could you tell at that distance?"

"I remembered the car. A 'seventy-seven Chrysler Imperial is kind of distinctive."

Three more cars passed.

"What if nobody will stop for us?" asked Acorn, beginning to look rather dismal.

"Oh dear, these clothes and our hair must be putting people off," said Gwen.

"Don't worry, somebody is sure to stop," Laura reassured them. "We just have to wait for a car chock full of kids and dogs and packages and people. They're the ones who stop and invite you to squeeze in. But anyway, it's getting late, and I think we should walk to the next bend and see what we can see. We may not be so very far from a house after all."

Around the bend there was a wondrous sight: some quarter of a mile down the road stood a gas station and a telephone booth.

"Bingo!"

"Eureka!"

"Thank goodness!"

"Goody goody gumdrops!"

"Perhaps it's one of my dad's," added Acorn, tagging after the others. "He owns an oil company."

When they reached the garage, they found, to everyone's dismay, that it was shut and empty.

"It must be after suppertime and they've all gone home, but at least there's a phone," said Harry. "Has anybody got a dime?" The extreme unlikelihood of this struck him immediately. He looked around, uncertain what to do next.

"You usually don't need a dime to dial nine-one-one," said Laura, who could be relied on for such practical knowledge. She lifted the receiver. No dial tone. She dialed the emergency number anyway. No answer. She put the phone down slowly. "I guess this is the kind that does need a dime," she said. Her eyes widened, appalled, as an all-too-familiar VW bus sped past on the other side of the road, stopped, and started to reverse, so that the rainbow was coming straight at them.

"Schleswig-Holstein, Omsk and Tomsk, Popacatapetl," chanted Harry.

"Poppy petal, Omsk, Tomsk," echoed Acorn.

"Chattanooga, Kalamazoo," Gwen chimed in.

"Vienna, Salzburg, London, Cardiff," tried Laura, who wasn't in the habit of using geography as magic, but had memorized her mother's itinerary.

As a charm, it worked spectacularly well. A pickup truck appeared from the opposite direction and slowed down alongside the frantically waving children.

"Need a ride, kids? Hop in." The driver started up again. "That guy sure looks mad," he said, glancing through his rearview mirror at Egbert, who was shaking his fist and bouncing with rage like an elongated tennis ball.

29

The driver of the pickup shook his head as he listened to the children's story, but whether it was in disbelief, or in disapproval of the Sharkes' villainy, was not clear.

"Look," he said at last, "I don't rightly know what to make of such goings on, but I have to be at my job at nine-thirty sharp. It's near that now, and a fire-watcher can't be a minute late tonight, so I'll have to drop you kids off in Minor Falls. The police station is in Basswood, but that's fifteen miles out of my way. It seems to me that the best thing is for you to get onto the phone to your folks."

He pulled up at a crossroads, in front of a small white church that had a sort of homemade spire rising from a roof of green asphalt tiles, and a faded sign saying PALESTINE LUTHERAN CHURCH.

"Reckon this is as good as anywhere. I turn off here for the forestry lookout post. Minor Falls is right over there." He jerked his head past the church.

"Just make for the water tower. You can't go wrong."

He gave them a dime for the phone and sped away to watch for forest fires, saying, "Have a good time now."

"He didn't believe us," said Harry slowly.

"Grownups usually only believe other grownups," observed Gwen.

Laura surveyed the Palestine Lutheran Church. It was a plain rectangular building whose only decoration was a semicircle of saw teeth over the door. Seen from underneath, the steeple looked like a conical hat perched on top of a garden trellis. She tried the door. Surprisingly, it was unlocked.

"I think you three should hide inside the church while I go and find a phone," she urged, although she didn't really want to go on alone. "Egbert is sure to be looking for us in Minor Falls by now, and there's no point in all of us asking to be caught."

Three rebellious faces looked back at her. Gwen gently shook her head. "Laura, now that we've come this far, I think we should go on sticking together," she said.

"Or the Sharkes may pick us off one by one," said Harry.

"I'm not staying behind," said Acorn.

"How about your heel, Laura? You can hardly walk." Gwen was concerned.

Laura took off her sneakers, laid them side by side on the church steps, and wriggled her toes in relief. "Who says I can't?" she challenged.

With a sudden sigh and a whoosh, an unexpected

huge Golden Chrysanthemum lit up the sky, followed by a rocket that whistled its way upward and exploded into three green stars.

"What's happening?" asked Acorn, alarmed. "Is it a war?"

"It must be the Fourth of July," said Laura. "Come on."

Followed by the others, she ran barefoot toward the noise. They passed the sign that welcomed them to Minor Falls, Population 327, and then the square, yellow-brick school, which had a fleet of five school buses parked in the gravel schoolyard. Over the brow of the hill they came to a gas station flying the American flag from a pole stuck in a gigantic tire. It too was closed. Ahead they could see the water tower, illuminated by the fireworks. It had "Go Cyclones" in large red letters on one silver side, and, under that, "Class of '81" in irregular blue letters. They came to a stop in the corner of a grassy square, jam-packed with people and vehicles of all shapes and sizes.

The children looked around in astonishment. They had been thinking of the North Woods as a wilderness, with few inhabitants, and certainly no friendly little towns like this one. Minor Falls seemed to have been planned on a grand scale by optimistic early settlers. There were buildings on three sides of the spacious square, which looked like a cross between a pasture and a baseball field. A railroad ran along the fourth side. Across the grass, a fire engine stood in readiness outside a whitewashed, concrete-block fire station, no bigger than a single-car garage. On

159

the side nearest to the children there was a row of shops. Outside the second store from the corner stood the very thing they needed, a public telephone booth.

The children headed straight for the phone, threading their way through the crowd and the scores of pickup trucks, motorbikes, campers, and cars. Everybody for miles around must have come to celebrate the Glorious Fourth in Minor Falls.

"I didn't think there were so many people in Minnesota," confided Jumping Green Mouse to High Silver Pine, who had tucked his hand in hers.

They skirted a particularly large, cheerful group. The grownups sat comfortably on folding aluminum chairs, handing around cans of beer, hot dogs, and corn chips, while the children ran about twirling luminous green batons and throwing firecrackers at one another.

"Laura is right," said Harry, coming to a stop. "There's no point in our all being conspicuous together. It would be safer for one person to go while the rest stay hidden, because Egbert will watch the phone if he has any sense."

Laura stooped and broke off a blade of grass. "The one who picks the grass does the phoning. Which hand?"

Gwen chose the empty hand. Laura shuffled the grass behind her back and held out her hands to Harry.

"Left." Harry always chose the left hand.

Laura opened her fist to show the grass crunched

inside. Harry was pleased and scared at the same time. Acorn pleaded to come along, but was persuaded to give his phone number instead. "Somebody always answers," he said. "If my father and mother are out, the butler or the housekeeper will be there."

Laura thought that sounded useful, if it was true. Everyone at the Washington number Harry's father had given him for emergencies might be out watching the fireworks. There was no one in her own apartment, and Gwen said her parents were on vacation.

"We can pretend to belong to this group, and stay here until you come back," Laura suggested. She edged Gwen and Acorn closer to where assorted relatives were shaking with laughter at an old family joke. One of them handed Gwen a hot dog.

"But . . ." began Gwen, embarrassed.

The stranger, however, had already turned to her sister to comment, "Must be Wilbur's youngest. I'd know that height anywhere."

Gwen divided her hot dog into three, and gave the others the larger pieces. Acorn rescued a discarded bag of tortilla chips. "My mother would be cross," he said, handing them around. "She doesn't like me to eat junk food, but I do it anyway," he admitted with a smile. "I even eat dog kibble, when no one's looking."

Laura was handed a bag of potato chips by a girl who said, "Want these? I can't stand sour cream and onion." Laura would have taken any flavor gladly. She shared it into four exactly equal portions, saving one for Harry.

Another adult threw them a blanket, saying, "Must be Norma's kids. She never did have an eye for clothes. Daft to let the girl go around with bare feet."

Laura gratefully pulled the cover over their three heads and shoulders. "I hope Harry is okay," she murmured, as they settled down to watch the fireworks from beneath the snug camouflage.

30

"Istanbul, Aberystwth." Harry made for the phone booth gripping his dime tightly, in case some stray firework startled him into dropping it. Feeling like a secret agent making his way through enemy country, he looked around for any sign of the Sharkes, and wondered again if they should have asked for help at one of the houses on the square, instead of trying to phone. Too late now. Anyway the houses would be empty tonight, and it wasn't easy to go up to strangers with a tale of phony camps and mass kidnapping. The forestry firewatcher had obviously thought they were exaggerating, and their clothes and haircuts weren't of a kind to inspire confidence. By this time, Harry was near enough to the phone booth to see that it was already occupied by a large woman in a purple flowered dress. He hoped her business wouldn't take long, and looked along the line of stores for a hiding place while he waited.

At the corner stood a grocery store with a large

Pepsi sign and a window full of cactus plants revealed by the orange glow from one of the few street lights and the flickering illumination of the fireworks. Next to the grocery store was a hardware store, which also served as the post office. Beyond that was Sue's Beauty Shop, then an empty store, then Bev's Café and Bar. On the far corner stood the Blue Skies Washeteria. Harry took cover in the doorway of the hardware store, opposite the telephone. He willed the purple-flowered lady to hurry up.

Harry shrank as far back into the shadows as he could, and kept a wary eye out for the Sharkes. Occasional glances at the window on his left revealed a jump rope with pink plastic handles resting against a set of wrenches. No sign of them yet. Harry directed burning messages toward the large lady's back.

"*Please* hurry," he urged.

The lady in the phone booth shifted to the other side, so Harry could see her face. She didn't look as though she was saying goodbye. Harry gave up and turned his attention to the cards taped to the shop door. He hadn't looked at them so far for fear he'd miss the instant when the phone became available, but it was nice to have something to read again, and at least it took his mind off the Sharkes for a moment. The 7TH ANNUAL MINOR FALLS FLEA MARKET was due on July 12. There was a CABIN FOR SALE ON PELICAN LAKE, and someone was offering CORDS OF HARDWOOD, CUT AND DELIVERED. Harry was just starting to read the lengthy catalogue of ANNA SWENSON: HOUSEHOLD EFFECTS, which were to be offered at auction next Saturday, when the woman in the phone booth hung up, gathered her coins and her purse, and opened the door.

Harry raced across the street. At the same time, three girls pushed past him squealing madly, chased by a group of boys with firecrackers. The girls dived into the booth and slammed the door. One boy tried to pry it open in order to throw a cracker inside. With shrieks and giggles, the girls held fast their fort.

Harry was desperate. "Excuse me," he said. "You have to get them out of there. I've got a call to make. It's a matter of life and death."

"Say," mocked the boy. "A matter of life and death." He tossed a firecracker in Harry's direction.

The girls shrieked some more and opened the door a crack to say, "We're never coming out of here, Clay Jensen, so there!"

The sky lit up with a shower of Golden Rain. As Harry looked around frantically for some other possibility, a warm, wet muzzle thrust itself into his hand. A sunburst of sparks went off, making the square as bright as day, and Harry saw the pale, ferrety face of Egbert Sharke staring straight at him through the window of Bev's Bar. The next moment he vanished in the dark.

"Off to fetch the others," thought Harry, giving up all hope of the phone booth. He ducked behind a nearby camper. Danger followed.

"Go home," Harry commanded.

Danger sniffed his pocket, wagging her tail in happy memory. Harry had an inspiration.

"Fetch," he said, lobbing an empty Coke can into the distance. Danger bounded off eagerly. Harry ran in the other direction, but stopped abruptly. Parked outside the Blue Skies Washeteria was the VW bus. Harry was glad to catch sight of a large dent in the rainbow. He doubled back the way he had come, and hid for a moment behind a row of propane-gas cylinders at the side of the grocery store.

The fireworks were coming thick and fast as the display worked up to the grand climax. By the rapid sequence of flashes he could see Coralene leaving the bus to join the hunt. He looked the other way. Egbert was coming toward him, Danger at his heels. Harry's heart thumped madly. He couldn't seem to get enough air.

"I can't let them catch me. The others are counting on me to get help," he told himself.

Harry doubted if any cries for aid would be noticed in the general bedlam of screams and shrieks that greeted the last and biggest round of fireworks. With a sinking heart, he realized that even a gunshot would sound entirely normal. His only hope was to run straight for the fire station. Why oh why hadn't they gone there first? He dodged across the road and crouched in the darkness between two cars, to catch his breath and determine the best moment for a run across the open grass.

The sky was crisscrossed with shooting stars as the most spectacular fireworks of all began to explode. The spectators breathed a collective "ooh" and started to applaud. The last stars dropped back to earth,

166

followed by a darkness that seemed doubly dense after the dazzle that had gone before.

Harry ran for dear life. There seemed to be a hitch in the proceedings. He was three-quarters of the way across the grass, thinking he might make it after all, when his luck turned and the reason for the darkness became apparent. The whole area sprang into brilliant clarity as the set piece, the grand finale with the American flag, sizzled into action. The stars and stripes illuminated Harry in red, white, and blue before he could reach the shelter of the far row of cars. The merciless light also revealed Danger loping after him, Egbert moving around to head him off, and the VW bus, driven no doubt by Coralene, drawing up beside the five whitewashed boulders outside the fire station.

Panting for breath, Harry stumbled into the shadow of a bulky, old-fashioned car. Danger flung herself enthusiastically on his heels, while Egbert approached from the rear, his white face made blue by the fireworks' light. Harry wondered how long an undersized, bookwormish kid could fend off a full-grown man.

Egbert advanced. His face flickered to red. He was grinning in anticipation of triumph. A drip fell from the end of his long red nose. As Harry felt all hope ebbing away, the car door beside him swung open and a firm hand pulled him to safety.

31

"Now, young man," said a pleasant, no-nonsense, elderly voice. "Suppose you lock the door on your side and tell me why you're playing hide-and-seek with those unsavory-looking people."

Harry found himself staring into a pair of piercing gray eyes, and an oddly familiar face that looked as if it was in the habit of being obeyed. His rescuer wore an ancient tweed fishing hat, from which her white hair, quite as uncontrollable as Laura's, escaped in every direction. She was sitting bolt upright in this unlikely sort of car. For one thing, Harry doubted his head would touch the roof if he stood upright, and for another, the rear seats seemed extraordinarily far away. The door handle behind Harry rattled insistently.

"Taxi! Taxi!" shrilled an all-too-well-known voice.

Harry slid to the floor, unpleasant shivers running down his spine.

"Open up, my good woman," the voice commanded. More rattling.

"Certainly not. This is a private car, ma'am, and I am about to depart. Would you be so good as to remove your hands, and permit me to reverse?"

Coralene Sharke poured through the window a flood of reasons why she had to find her darling nephew, who, it seemed, had measles and was extremely contagious and delirious as well. He was probably babbling all sorts of nonsense that mustn't be believed for one moment.

"It is most careless of you, ma'am, to have mislaid a boy in that condition," responded Harry's rescuer, unmoved. "Kindly restrain your dog from slobbering on my windows."

With that, they sailed off majestically, the driver looking neither to the right, where Coralene was trying to open the car door, nor to the left, where Egbert was gesticulating madly.

"Tiresome people," she commented. "You can get up from the floorboards now, and tell me where you'd like to go, young man."

"Well, I have to find the others first."

"And pray how many of you are there?" inquired his rescuer.

"Only four," Harry reassured her.

"Then by all means direct me to the spot where you've stowed your friends. I no longer turn my head with comfort, so I shall rely on you to warn me of pursuit."

Harry turned to search for the bus. The Sharkemobile, he was delighted to see, was completely boxed in. Every driver in the place had apparently decided that now the show was over, it was time to go home. There was no possible way Egbert could extricate his bus from the traffic gridlock.

Laura was standing with Gwen and Acorn where Harry had left them, looking rather forlorn. She followed Harry to what she recognized as an old Checker cab, and climbed into the back with a questioning look on her face. Acorn was so delighted to sit on the jump seat that he forgot to be mystified.

"Jumping Green Mouse," he chanted happily to himself as he bounced up and down. "Jump, jump, Jumping Green Mouse."

"Shh," said Gwen. "Try being Silent Green Mouse."

"If you have nothing better to suggest," said their champion, "I think we should go back to my house. There are umpteen infuriating roadblocks, for some reason I cannot fathom, but I think we can avoid them. I know the side roads around here rather well. Then, over supper, you shall explain why four children, with no apparent parental supervision, are playing prisoner's base with some disreputable adults in Minor Falls, Minnesota, on the Fourth of July."

Over supper of steaming hot soup, with noodles and beans and peapods and leeks and carrots (Laura even thought she found some radish), and all the warm, crusty, homemade bread they could eat—which was a remarkable amount—the children explained.

"There is one question that still bothers me," their hostess said at last. "Why do Harry and Laura remind

170

me so strongly of my own family—my nephews, to be precise?''

There was a perplexed silence. Laura's mind worked quickest. "Steven and Henry Lewis! Our fathers! You must be Great-Aunt Adelaide!" she cried joyfully. "I knew that dreadful Coralene couldn't really be our aunt. You always said that, Gwen, didn't you?"

"Explain, please, Gwen—what did you always say?''

A little later, Great-Aunt Adelaide said, "Dear me. What impostors. Worse than anything Nellie Highly dreamed up. I suppose that if I hadn't isolated myself so completely up here, I might have prevented all this. I rarely get mail of any interest nowadays, so I pick it up only once a month. There was a letter from your mother, Laura, which made so little sense to me that yesterday I went over to Nish Na Bosh Na myself. It must have been just after you had gone. However, it is an ill wind that blows no good. The breeze fanned by those unmentionable Sharkes has blown me some most agreeable relatives and guests.''

"Well, well," she said, stacking the soup bowls, "only ten days ago I was persuaded to install one of Alexander Graham Bell's contraptions. It looks as if it may yet prove its worth. I had better start sending some telegrams and making some calls. Now what was that number again, Acorn?"

32

Acorn's parents were the first to arrive. A chauffeur accompanied them, carrying the Nice-and-Cosy in gloved hands.

"My darling baby, how can I ever bear to let you out of my sight again?" cried Molly Oakes, clasping Acorn so tightly that his nose was squashed against a gold button on her coat. A moment later she was holding him at arm's length to inspect the damage. "Whatever has happened to your beautiful curls? That terrible, terrible blackmailing photograph was really you. Oh, my poor snuggy-pooh." Acorn was squeezed against the buttons once more.

"Now sit down, everyone, and start at the beginning. I want to hear the whole story," instructed the richest man on the eastern seaboard.

"Well, I'll be darned," he said at last. "That camp had such a great reputation in the thirties. Adelaide Lewis is one of the all-time greats in education. Up there with Dewey, my father always said."

Great-Aunt Adelaide raised one skeptical eyebrow.

"Acorn's grandfather, Ames Oakes the Third, used to say that some of the happiest days of his life were spent at Nish Na Bosh Na. He always regretted the place's closing, so that I could never follow in his footsteps, so to speak. When I saw the camp was re-opening for one season, I thought it would be just the ticket for Acorn. He was a bit young, but his mother tends to baby the lad. I thought he could do with a spot of toughening up."

"Toughening up," moaned Molly Oakes, running her hands through Acorn's shorn locks.

"They sent no end of fine references," said her husband defensively.

"That'd be Egbert," explained Laura.

"Forged, eh? My lawyers should have spotted that."

"I remember Oakey," said Great-Aunt Adelaide. "A tiresome boy who always wanted to play trains."

"Did he now?" Mr. Oakes was interested, rather than offended, by this light on his parent. "I guess that was because the family fortunes were founded on railways. The Ames Oakes clan are loyal to a fault: trains, Nish Na Bosh Na, and so on."

"Darling," said Mrs. Oakes, looking at the grungy blanket that Acorn had taken from the chauffeur with a delighted smile. "Mommy will buy you another Nice-and-Cosy, if we have to ransack New York. I dare say Halston would make you a lovely replica. This old one is really worn out, and I shall never forget that terrible moment when your father brought it into the Basswood police station. My nerves were shattered."

Acorn clutched his comforter tighter and edged nearer Gwen. This was not missed by Great-Aunt Adelaide. "I think you should remember," she said a little sternly, "that Acorn's chronological age may be seven, but from what I hear of the way he kept up with the older children, his emotional age is now a good deal more. He's capable of making his own decisions."

Molly Oakes looked startled. Acorn whispered shyly to Gwen, who said something in turn to Aunt Adelaide.

"Of course you may come and visit us," said the great educator promptly. "In fact, since I seem to be running an unexpected summer camp at my advanced age, I think you should return for a day or two before the end of the summer, to see what Camp Nish Na Bosh Na should have been like."

Acorn accepted enthusiastically. Mrs. Oakes looked very doubtful, but her husband said, "Very handsome of you. His grandfather would be most pleased. Always said Nish Na Bosh Na was the making of him, you know."

As the Ames Oakeses left in the waiting Rolls, the one-and-only, original Nice-and-Cosy tucked firmly under Acorn's arm, the telegraph boy cycled up, dodging around a birch tree to avoid the impressive car.

"Gee willikers," he said, catching sight of the uniformed chauffeur. "Things are certainly hopping in the North Woods this year. Telegram for Laura Lewis from Austria," he announced at the cabin door.

174

"Glad you folks are at home. Not like my last trip."

Laura opened the envelope and read, A LITTLE NIGHT MUSIC MARVELOUS IN SALZBURG VIENNA NEXT GLAD AUNT ADELAIDE FOUND WAS SHE LOST WHAT FUSS PLEASE EXPLAIN HAVE RECEIVED NO MAIL SINCE CHANGING ITINERARY LOVE LYDIA.

"Just like Mother," said Laura. "I'm glad she's safe, but she really does need a manager."

From somewhere near Tahiti, a message was taken to New Zealand by special courier, flashed by satellite to Washington, and beamed from there to a secret post near the Canadian border. An unobtrusive man in a raincoat arrived at the cabin next morning to check on Harry's safety.

"I think you're a little late on the job, young man. Where was your organization when my great-nephew needed you?" asked Great-Aunt Adelaide rather severely. "Now that you're here, you can make yourself useful by collecting a pair of shoes that are sitting on the steps outside the Palestine Lutheran Church in Minor Falls."

It wasn't the usual sort of secret mission, but the agent did it anyway. Aunt Adelaide had that sort of authority.

"Wouldn't you say he's locking the stable after the horse has gone?" said Gwen, smiling, from the stove where she was stirring the chokecherry jelly.

"A sensible child," said Aunt Adelaide approvingly. "I'm glad we thought of asking your parents to agree to your staying with me for the rest of the summer. I need someone to balance all these great-nieces and great-nephews I've just acquired, especially someone who can collect enough chokecherries for jelly and who knows how to make sassafras tea."

Gwen beamed.

"I would've thought your smiles were rusty, you used them so little," teased Morning Star.

"I didn't have anything to smile about until now," replied High Silver Pine.

33

BABES OUT OF THE WOODS

The headline spread right across the front page of the Basswood newspaper. For once, the photographs of the fireworks at Minor Falls were relegated to the back page, by the report that the missing campers had been found on a remote lake by Environmental Protection Agency scientists sampling water acidity in the Boundary Waters. The entire inside fold was filled with pictures of the derelict cabins at Nish Na Bosh Na.

The *Northern Light* reporter finally got her scoop.

"NOTHING" SAYS CORALENE SHARKE

"Much ado about nothing," said Mrs. Coralene Sharke, when interviewed by our reporter in the traditional Fourth of July traffic jam outside the fire station in Minor Falls.

Mrs. Sharke, who refused to give her age, was dressed in a magenta chiffon holiday creation of her own design.

MISUNDERSTANDING

Sharke explained that the whole thing had been an unfortunate misunderstanding. Her sister, Miss Diana-Discipline Sharke, 50, had allegedly taken the "little darlings" on an extended overnight. We are informed she was running the controversial Camp Nish Na Bosh Na according to the latest survival-course theories.

DOSE OF SALT

"Children have no sense of proportion," said Mrs. Sharke, when asked about the extraordinary statements made by the rescued campers. "And no sense of humor at all. You have to take them with a dose of salt."

SOUTH AMERICA NEXT

"No comment," was Mr. Egbert Sharke's reply to every question put by our reporter. However, we understand that Coralene Sharke, escorted by her brother, plans an extensive South American vacation tour. Mrs. Sharke regretted that she could not at this point in time give our readers the precise itinerary. "Everyone likes to get away from it all now and again," she commented with a charming smile.

Miss D-D Sharke is thought to be interviewing for a job as coach to the Costaraguan Olympic team.

(*Editor's note:* The above world-exclusive was secured by our alert reporter at yesterday's festivities in Minor Falls, shortly before all members of the Sharke family disappeared from the area. We understand that the FBI is extremely anxious to interview the Sharkes on charges of kidnapping, extortion, misrepresentation, breaking the health and juvenile-employment laws, and some forty-one other charges. Will any person with knowledge of their whereabouts please contact their nearest police station immediately.)

34

Hiking around Lake Nish Na Bosh Na on Labor Day in search of the wild sarsaparilla, Aunt Adelaide told Gwen, who had stayed behind an extra week when the others left, "From what you say about your parents' demanding jobs, my dear, you are in need of a summer home. I can see how much you like the North Woods, so if you can put up with an opinionated old woman, you're welcome to stay here each year as long as you want. Judging by the last few weeks, I think we might deal very comfortably together. I watched you with the little Oakes boy, and think you have the makings of a first-rate teacher. In fact, you could come before the regular vacation; I've made sure that the local school maintains a reasonable standard of old-fashioned excellence."

Gwen nodded, too happy to be able to find the right words.

"Well, I'm glad that's settled," said the famous educator, leading the way into a green tunnel through the trees. She stopped to point out the heart-shaped leaves of a ginger plant and to comment on the glancing pattern of light: "'Glory be to God for dappled things.' Do you know the poem?"

Gwen shook her head.

"No? I shall have to teach you some Hopkins, one of the very best nineteenth-century poets, I think. Schools pay far too little attention to learning poetry by heart nowadays. After all, one must have some mental furniture."

Gwen felt a little dizzy at the level of the conversation. She hoped she wouldn't prove a disappointment. Harry had given her his tree book; perhaps she should have asked him for a reading list as well.

"Well," said her companion briskly, "we shall have a lot more to do than brew sassafras tea, now that I've been able to buy the entire lake and a good portion of the surrounding forest, with the kind assistance of Mr. Dubious. Did you know that he was so anxious to obtain a small plot of land I owned between Minor Falls and Little Fool Lake that he offered me the whole of Nish Na Bosh Na in exchange? So unlike the man to cheat himself, rather than others. Such a greedy family. I never knew whether the Highlys or the Dubiouses were the worst. A most suitable marriage, of course; they deserve each other. What young James did not realize at the time, I fancy, is that I had already sold a part of the land to Minor Falls, as a site for their new sewage plant—the one that's replaced all the haphazard sewer drainage into Lake Nish Na Bosh Na."

A pleased smile transformed Miss Lewis's normally stern features, and then a chuckle escaped her as she thought how peeved Nellie Highly would be to hear this news.

Gwen suddenly realized what she had been missing: the smell. A pleasant breeze was blowing off the water, bringing freshness and the thought of sailboats, in place of wafts of dead fish and rotten eggs.

"Mr. Oakes sent me a most generous check, and so I plan to turn the whole area into a nature preserve, and to rebuild Camp Nish Na Bosh Na," Aunt Adelaide continued. "Laura and Harry insist they're coming back every summer to assist, and I wouldn't be surprised if his father wants young Acorn to come."

Gwen had never dreamed she could look out over the waters of Lake Nish Na Bosh Na feeling quite so happy.

In Basswood, Mr. James Dubious said to his wife, "If only that old cow had stayed in the backwoods, we would be sitting on a bundle now."

It was not clear to whom he was referring, but Mrs. Dubious tapped him playfully on the lips and cooed, "My, my, watch your language, Pootsie."

In Minneapolis, a VW bus that had been abandoned in the airport parking lot was turned over to the Salvation Army. They repainted the rainbow and found it invaluable in their good works.

In New York, Molly Oakes said, "Oakey, do you think we should have a psychiatrist look at Acorn? I hadn't thought the precious pet was any the worse for that dreadful time in Minnesota this summer, but now I fear the damage may have gone deep. He keeps saying 'Omsk' and 'Tomsk.' Aren't they in Russia? The other day he was talking about Chimborazo, wherever that might be. And he refers to himself as Jumping Green Mouse, you know."

"I wouldn't let it bother you," said his father. "A little geography may be a good thing. I'll get him a globe. Just keep an eye on him. He did mention something about a high silver pine to me. We were in the elevator. No trees anywhere."

In Washington, Ames Oakes the Fourth called on Harry, who was reading a book about otters. "I've got a four-star general's hat for you, my boy. Acorn told me you liked that sort of thing, and I'm not without influence at the Pentagon. We owe you, and that cousin of yours, a lot, you know."

Harry thanked him politely and hung the cap on the wall. He quite liked having it there, but he never wore it.

In Chicago, Laura and her mother were together again.

"Laura dear," said her mother. "Do you think we should get you some voice lessons? You used to speak so clearly, but now you mumble, so that I've hardly understood a word you've said all fall."

"It's okay, Mom," said Laura, without moving her lips. "I'm practicing to be a famous ventriloquist. How do you like Morning Star as a stage name?"